CREATING
EDEN

THE GARDEN
AS A HEALING SPACE

Marilyn Barrett, Ph.D.

HarperSanFrancisco
An Imprint of HarperCollins*Publishers*

Library of Congress Cataloging-in-Publication Data

Barrett, Marilyn.
  Creating Eden: the garden as a healing space / Marilyn Barrett.—1st ed.
  Includes bibliographical references.
    ISBN 0–06–250076–7 (cloth)
    ISBN 0–06–250091–0 (pbk.)
    1. Gardening—Therapeutic use. I. Title.
RM735.7.G37B37   1992
615.8'515—dc20   635.01 Gdn. philosophy   91–55317

96 97 98 99 00 ICC\RRD(H) 10 9 8 7 6 5 4 3 2 1

THIS BOOK IS DEDICATED
TO THE MEMORY OF MY MOTHER,
Ruth Weil Klein,
AND MY FATHER,
Leo Klein

CONTENTS

ACKNOWLEDGMENTS

I WOULD LIKE to thank Natasha Kern, my literary agent, for believing in this project in its early stages.

My deepest appreciation goes to writing consultant Dorothy Wall, who helped me find the voice I needed to transform my doctoral dissertation into a book for the general reader. She opened a door to self-expression for which I shall always be grateful.

Barbara Moulton, my editor at Harper San Francisco, offered enthusiastic support, intelligent critique, and helpful suggestions as she skillfully shepherded *Creating Eden* through the publishing process. I feel fortunate to have worked with her.

Editorial assistant Barbara Archer deserves recognition for her friendly manner and prompt replies to my questions. My gratitude also to Noreen Norton, my production editor, for her calm and good humor as she efficiently guided my book from final manuscript to printed page.

Art director Jamie Sue Brooks orchestrated the design and art for *Creating Eden;* its handsome appearance is a testament to her skill and talent.

Kathleen Edwards's lovely illustrations add a visual dimension to *Creating Eden* that is delightful and very much in keeping with the spirit of the book.

Thanks also to Sylvia Elber, Jennifer Barrett, Celia Callender, Judy Ziegler, Jenny Newton, Jennifer Charnofsky, Aileen Vance, Susan Stone, Les Gripkey, and David and

Freda Mallen for their friendship, comments, ideas, and continuing interest during the writing of this book.

For help with resources and information for the bibliography and appendix, I wish to acknowledge Dr. Diane Relf, Dr. Mark Francis, Vivian Gratton, and Gary Appel.

INTRODUCTION

COME INTO THE GARDEN with me. Don't worry about not knowing the way: Your heart remembers, even if your head has forgotten. When you were small and first had time to create your dreams, you were at one with the earth you played in and with each leaf, bird, and cloud you saw. This is the garden to which I invite you to return.

Imagine a place to which you can bring stress, sorrow, loneliness, and confusion and from which you can leave with a sense of resolution, understanding, and calm. Imagine a place where you can express your own unique nature, create beauty, grow pure food, and gain control over your life. In my life, the garden has been such a place.

As I learned of the garden's power to heal and renew, I not only moved through and resolved a serious health crisis but also brought harmony and balance into my life. I let go of many "shoulds" and "oughts" and began to live a life closer to my true inner needs and to the natural world of which I am a part.

My purpose in writing this book is to share what I have learned. Gardening is a healing art, both physically and spiritually, and once you learn its principles, you, too, will be able to develop and maintain a way of life that is in harmony with your own inner nature and with Nature around you.

Is much of your life determined by others' needs? Are you just getting by? Do you have a nagging feeling that something is wrong, that from the time you were little you have been swept along, marching to someone else's beat, never having the time or the tools to figure out what is really right for you?

Or are you feeling burned out and tired of the rat race—as though you have been running on a treadmill, achieving the illusion of progress and happiness but not really feeling good deep within you?

That's the way it was for me. It was only in retrospect, after things began to come apart and I became ill, that I saw how out of balance my life was with my own true nature.

The crisis of my illness and my desire to get well enabled me to see that my real wants and needs, my true, essential spirit, my very self had been covered over by layers and layers of stress, disappointment, and compromise. I no longer remembered what it was that I wanted and needed to be happy. I decided to try to rediscover it.

I left my job in a smoggy, semidesert town and moved to Los Angeles, where I bought a house two miles from the ocean. The house had a large, denuded backyard littered with broken glass, dead weeds, and rubble. Except for one or two shrubs and a small clump of birches, the space, which was about half the size of an average city house lot, was barren. Yet the soil was heavy clay, and I could see that with some attention it could become good garden loam.

Guided by visions that I'd had in my mind since childhood, I decided to create my own garden space. I hauled away the trash, uprooted dead plants, cleared weeds, and enriched the soil. The garden evolved as I went along. Generous neighbors donated calla lilies, iris, impatiens, and Mexican evening primrose. As houses in the neighborhood were demolished to make way for condominiums, I rescued from the bulldozers violets, tiger lilies, geraniums, roses, and fuchsias. Bricks for walkways I retrieved from the same sites. Each day I spent time in the garden digging, planting, and weeding, adding cosmos, lobelia, calendula, and forget-me-nots to the beds and borders I created.

As I dug and planted, I began to get in touch with the strength in my body and to feel the benefits of being out of doors. My energy began to return, and my depression lifted.

Working in the garden that first year, clearing and planting, I discovered that I was also working out the answers to many questions and problems. As my garden began to take tentative shape, my psyche, too, began to form an image of where I was in my life. As drooping irises, calla lilies, and sword ferns survived the shock of transplanting and as earthworms multiplied in the soil that I dug and fertilized, I gained comfort and release from some of the fear and uncertainty I felt. Then, later, as these plants took root and sent out new green shoots, as I dug borders and laid out pathways, some impending shape of my own future began to emerge within me. In spring, when the tall callas unfurled their creamy blooms and the jowled and ruffled heads of blue and yellow irises opened from tightly sheathed buds, as flowers and leaves stirred and rustled in the gentle, sun-warmed breeze and as lemon blossoms from a small tree I'd planted in autumn scented the air, I saw that I, too, had completed a cycle of growth.

Through this connectedness with the rhythms of Nature, I gained balance and perspective and was able to see just how distanced from my needs I had become.

So it is for many of us. So it is with the planet. The stresses we face force us to violate and become alienated from our own basic human needs. Daily we hear of global warming, the greenhouse effect, and the destruction of the ozone layer. We have become unable to regulate our outer environment as well as our inner environment.

This book will show you how to restore and maintain a healthful connection with Nature and with yourself. It will help you to reduce stress, feel more content, and come to know your personal boundaries and limits of tolerance.

You will learn to use the actual garden, in your back or front yard, on your balcony or windowsill. And you will also learn how to create and use a mental garden, one you can carry with you and that will help you to restore and retain your balance as you move through your daily life.

Why the garden? It is immediate and tangible—it's not an idea, or a theory, or an abstraction. It is a microcosm of Nature's processes, a little world you can make on your own human scale. In the garden, you can learn to flow with the rhythms of Nature; you can attune yourself to Nature's harmony.

The garden is a place where you can, literally and figuratively, come to your senses and find delight in them. The seasons are dependable guides from which we can learn to lead a wise and thoughtful life.

Perhaps after a hard winter that you thought would never end, from a bare tree branch you'd swear was dead, a small bud bursts into being. Suddenly your own hope is renewed. You feel affirmed, feel you can do it, too, spring back to life when you've been in the deep freeze. This feeling doesn't come from watching television, or eating TV dinners, or working in an office with fluorescent lights and no windows.

All gardeners know that in some way they "work out their problems in the garden." There is no mystery to it. They are simply following Nature's laws.

This book explores ways in which you can make sense of your problems, zero in on areas of stress and dysfunction in your life, and then restore your life balance by exploring the mental and physical garden activities described in the chapters that follow.

Remember that how you approach your garden is even more important than what you accomplish in it. Particularly if you're a person who is under a great deal of stress, you may initially want to use your garden simply as a place where you can sit and rest. The garden tasks can wait until you're ready.

In the process of making and enjoying your garden, you will learn to make your life more manageable, your work more meaningful. You will find ways to deal with loneliness, grief, and relationships, and you will feel better about yourself.

Come into the garden with me. Follow me now on a journey through Nature's ways. Smell the dampness of the soil, the scent of the flowers, observe the birds and insects. Feel the breeze on your face and listen as it stirs the tree branches. Soak in the warmth of the sun. Hold the soil in your hands and renew your connection with the earth. Pay full attention to what really matters within and around you. Say "yes" to being fully alive and at one with everything in the garden that is your life.

1

MIND GARDENS

*All my life through, the new sights of
Nature made me rejoice like a child.*

MARIE CURIE

HOW CAN YOU ESCAPE the numbing effects of noise, crowds, plastics, fluorescent lights, airless offices, and shopping malls? Where can you find respite from the demands on you as you hurry to meet work or school deadlines, cope with a crying child, care for an aging parent, or try to resolve an argument that you've had with your spouse or roommate? You can go to the garden, an imaginary garden you create in your mind.

I'm going to guide you back to a place in which you can experience more fully what you feel, see, taste, touch, and hear. Here you will find peace and a place to rest. You will have an opportunity to look around you, to create, and simply to be. You will open into a world in which you can hear the sounds of birds, inhale fresh, clear air, soak in the warmth of the sun, bite into a crisp apple or a vine-ripened tomato you've grown, or listen to the peaceful trickle of water from a fountain. Here you will move slowly, always aware of your breath, your movement, at one with your basic nature and the world of Nature around you. You will open like a flower. In your garden, you yourself will bloom.

Don't worry about not having enough time—there will be enough. Don't worry about what you are leaving behind—you will be able to return when you need to.

When I speak to you of balance and harmony, I'm talking about living within your breath, living within your natural rhythm. Do that for a moment—just breathe, listening to the rise and fall of your breath. Listen to it for the next few minutes.

Allow your thoughts to flow; don't fight them. Instead, focus your attention on your breathing, feeling it slow as you relax. Observe your thoughts as they arise, then return to your breathing—knowing that this is your nature, that you are returning to your natural rhythm.

Many of us are out of breath, pushed by the pace at which we're forced to live. Mind gardening is something you can do to counteract this breathlessness and the stress and disharmony that go with it.

Get into a comfortable, relaxed position. Loosen or remove constricting clothing or jewelry. Settle into your body as you focus on your breathing. As you inhale and exhale, imagine your breath to be a gently blowing wind. Allow this gentle wind to soften your rib cage and expand your chest cavity from your shoulders to your stomach as you breathe in and out.

Now you are going to relax your body by tensing and relaxing each muscle group. Make fists of your hands. Clench them as tightly as possible, holding that position until you count to three, and then let your fists relax. Now, one by one, focus on the muscles in the rest of your body—your feet, legs, buttocks, stomach, shoulders, arms, back, neck, and face—tensing each group of muscles one at a time, holding until you count to three, and then relaxing.

Remember to continue your relaxed breathing. Become aware of any remaining tension in your body and send your breath to that particular place, asking that part to relax. Allow your breath to clear a restful space inside of you, as you inhale and exhale with the rhythm of a gently blowing breeze.

As you continue to breathe, imagine yourself going to a place that has been given to you where you can make a garden. To get there, you may walk down a city street, or down a hallway to a balcony, or climb a stairway to a rooftop. Or perhaps you travel down a country road or follow a path through a forest.

Imagine yourself arriving at this place where you will make your garden. Take a look around you. Are you in the backyard of a house in the city? Are you on a hillside with a view or in a valley looking up at the mountains? How large is your garden space? What's around it? Is there a house next door, or are you alone in an open landscape? Is the ocean nearby?

What kind of soil is there? Is it ready for planting, or do you need to dig and enrich it, clear rocks and tree stumps before you can plant? Think about the size and shape you want your garden to be. You may or may not want paths, fountains, or walkways. Will you make it rectangular, circular, or do you want the shape to emerge as you make the garden? Do you want a formal garden with manicured borders and neatly planted rows of flowers and plants? Or do you want it to be wild and natural? What is the water source, and how will it reach the plants?

If you are feeling tired, stressed, and overworked, you may want a garden that frees you from obligation—one in which you don't have to do much work or one that will maintain itself as Nature maintains itself. A garden planted with drought-tolerant plants will conserve your energy just as it conserves the earth's resources. A garden using plants native to your locale will require less tending. Or you may find planning and planting a more elaborate garden a creative and relaxing outlet in which your contact with the plants and soil invigorates and renews you.

You may plant trees for shade or fruit depending on what kind of garden you want, for you can have anything in this space. What plants and flowers would you like? Do you want to put in flowers from a garden you remember from the past? Perhaps ones from your childhood that you gathered and made into nosegays? Or plants you recall from a favorite park or botanical garden? You may choose flowers in your favorite colors: purple violets, pansies, and crocuses; blue lobelia; pink roses and azaleas; orange poppies and yellow daffodils. Or would you like exotic flowers such as orchids and gardenias? Perhaps you'd like grapes and wisteria to climb an arbor for shade in summer. Or you may put in a cactus garden. What bushes and shrubs? Rhododendrons and lilacs to flower in the spring? Hibiscus for summer? A shed for tools and a place to sit? Or some garden statuary? Whatever you choose will be right for you.

Take a last stroll through your garden. As you leave, look around, surveying in detail what you have envisioned. If you would like to and if it feels right, give a name to this garden space.

You may find it difficult in the beginning, in the midst of stress and turmoil, to remember that your garden is there waiting for you when you need it. The name you have given this space can lead you back to it.

This is your garden sanctuary. It belongs to you alone. It is a place that you can visit any time you want. You can take it with you wherever you go. In order to enjoy a respite from stress and to restore your inner balance, you need only remember that it is there.

2

CLEARING

*The art of life lies in the constant
readjustment to our surroundings.*

KAKUZO OKAKURA

ACH PERSON'S IDEA OF a garden is unique. In creating a garden, we not only open a door to Nature but to an ideal space, one we can control and order.

For some, this may mean creating a formal design in which plants and shrubs are carefully placed and trimmed, where meticulous attention is paid to each detail and deviation from the original garden plan is discouraged. For others who prefer a sense of the wild and natural, less control may be exercised. Yet all gardens need to be maintained in order for our original intention, whether planned or spontaneous, to emerge. One of the most important maintenance activities is clearing.

Through many seasons and years of gardening, I have come to realize that there are various kinds of clearing: clearing to make a new garden, seasonal clearing, and ongoing maintenance.

Clearing to Make a New Garden

Creating a new garden presents us with a myriad of choices. The first choice, whether the plot has been gardened before or not, is to decide what to leave and what to take out.

I've made several new gardens over the past twenty years. I remember once inheriting a garden in which a tall, long-needled pine tree dominated the site and cast deep shade over most of it. At first I felt dismay at its presence, for I knew that sun-loving garden favorites such as roses and bougainvillea would not survive in its shadow.

Still, it was a beautiful tree and attracted many birds. I decided to design a shade garden with the tree as the centerpiece. In spring I planted Australian tree ferns, pink rhododendrons, and azaleas, then added violets, primroses, cinerarias, and irises in shades of pink, blue, and purple. In summer I added impatiens in various shades of pink, together with multicolored fuchsia, then maidenhair fern and a ground cover of baby's tears.

In the heat of summer, this shaded space became a cool haven of rest and peace. When I think of it today, I recall the smell of moist soil and pine needles, the soft glow of shaded light on stem, flower, bud, and leaf.

When you begin to create your new garden, you must take care to respect the preexisting vegetation. Take your cue from Nature and keep whatever possible of the original landscape.

A clump of birch trees, a palm, or some birds of paradise already standing could become the focal point of the garden you make. Large stones might be left in place and incorporated into the landscape design.

Think carefully before you eliminate established plantings. They may not have been those you'd have planted, but you can't easily replace them. Reflect on each plant or shrub. Think of how many seasons it has taken for its trunk and limbs to mature, how long it has taken for its roots to reach deep beneath the soil.

A small seedling planted by a gardener a generation or two ago, if wisely chosen and thoughtfully placed, may grow into a large and graceful tree that provides shade, a place for birds to nest and for children to climb and play. In this way, gardeners of the past reach out to us through time.

I've seen people bulldoze all of the established shrubs in a garden only to learn the hard way, after they have denuded the space, that it will take a long time for new trees and shrubs to sink roots, branch out, and flower.

Aren't our relationships like that, too? They need time to sink roots and deepen. When we think only of our immediate needs and act thoughtlessly and impulsively toward those we care about, we may damage trust and intimacy developed over months and years. We need to accept and value the "givens" and to work with and around them.

While we want to save that which is valuable as we begin to make a new garden, there may also be much that needs to be cleared. In making my shade garden with the large pine, I had first to clear away debris left by the previous gardener. Dead branches littered the ground under the tree, and some shriveled and mildewed plants had to be removed.

We may find the garden spaces we inherit overgrown and neglected. Trash and broken glass may litter the ground. Trees and shrubs may be diseased, dead, or too large for the site. In order to make our garden, it is necessary for us to remove them and clear away the debris.

As you make your new garden, look around to see what you'll need to clear. Perhaps you'll need to clear old leaves or litter, perhaps old lumber, broken pipe, and diseased plants. You'll also want to pull out roots and stumps that will interfere with your own garden.

For those who come from chaotic or troubled families, which can be likened to sad, untended gardens, clearing away anger, confusion, and pain, the "trash" of the past, is a prerequisite to achieving inner peace, balance, and harmony. These people must first sort through the emotional rubble of the past they have inherited, and they must get to the roots of attitudes and behavior patterns that have stunted their growth. This process allows them then to restore foundations and clear new ground for gardens that can flourish.

It is important not to live with old problems. If a tree has grown too large and its roots reach under the house and threaten the foundation, it must be removed. Otherwise it will continue to be a problem no matter how beautiful it is.

On occasion, we'll find a tree or shrub in our garden that has been leveled to the ground, but the stump is left. This could be a lovely remainder, a place where children might have a tea party, but more often it presents an obstacle and needs to be removed.

Old deep roots must be extracted, for they may grow back. Also, it will be difficult for anything new to root and grow in the space where stumps and roots remain.

We see this paralleled in life as we observe ourselves or others allowing problems to "grow back." Alcoholics who sober up only to relapse periodically, smokers and users of other drugs who quit only to begin again are people who are "stumped," who have been unable to root out the cause of their self-destructive behaviors.

When Roseanne, a woman in her early thirties, came to see me, she was in the throes of a depression brought on by the ending of her third marriage. She felt a sense of despair and failure in her inability to have a successful relationship. As we discussed her situation, she began to see that there was a pattern to her series of failed marriages. Each of her partners had been at least twenty years her senior and although initially attentive and loving, each had become abusive and neglectful, abandoning her within a year of marriage.

In recounting her family history, Roseanne disclosed that when she was two years old, her father had deserted her and her mother and had made no attempt to contact either of them again. Through her therapy sessions, Roseanne was able to see how her unconscious needs for her father caused her to seek out older men who would repeat her early abandonment.

She was then able to give voice to the rage and sorrow she had been containing for so many years and thus to break the destructive pattern. Now she's able to catch herself when she falls into this pattern and ask herself whether it's what she really wants. This kind of self-awareness and self-control comes from getting to the root of our behaviors and from "clearing" the pain and anger of the past.

When you clear, be sure that you are not just doing so to recreate what you've seen at a friend's house or in a magazine. Sometimes people have an idea of a garden they've seen elsewhere. They hastily clear everything away and spend a lot of money on new plants in their attempt to replicate what they have seen.

Without the necessary understanding of how things grow, of what a garden needs, and of the special contours of their own unique space, these people are left with a hodge-podge of mismatched plants and landscaping. In such a garden, there can be no sense of organic unity.

We see this often in society: People who lack insight into their own needs and have no confidence in their own judgment will follow the latest fad, futilely superimposing mass-market ideals of beauty or success on themselves, often with disastrous results.

Rather than seeing the land as a means to an end, we must view it as a friend, and any clearing we undertake must foster the mutual respect and affection we wish to find in such a relationship. In this way we reinforce a fact that is easily overlooked in this technological age—that we and Nature are interdependent.

Seasonal Clearing

Spring. The garden calls and guides my eye to the earth.

Blue and white crocuses are first to break through the hard soil, and yellow blossoms of bare-branched forsythia array themselves against the gray monochrome of winter.

In the flower bed, I stoop and clear away layers of old, wet leaves blown in by winter storms. I lift them gently with my gloved hand and uncover tender daffodil and tulip shoots—green surprises from the cold earth.

Some things don't survive the winter. A weakened shrub or tree fails to leaf out, and I must clear it. Again I ask, what to save and what to let go? There are those who feel that everything they plant must have a permanent place in the garden. I am not that kind of gardener. I remove plants that do not thrive in my garden environment. I get rid of those with unpleasant habits that are not compatible with other plants. When morning glories that I love become garden pests, rampantly reseeding themselves and choking out other plants in my small garden space, I pull them out.

To make room for the new, I need to clear out what didn't work, what didn't give back to me, what didn't thrive.

The same is true in our lives. We need to sort through relationships, keep and cherish those that are fruitful, and clear away the ones that don't nourish us.

Just as we must remove a broken limb, a twisting vine, a diseased shrub that threatens the harmony and integrity of our garden, so by will and decision we must shut out a person or idea dangerous to our balance.

In autumn I clear away dead annuals and cut back leggy perennials so that they will grow fuller and flower abundantly in spring. To do this, I have to sacrifice the last of the flowers. The garden looks barren.

But many seeds have fallen to the ground from the dead flower heads, and small, dark seeds of forget-me-nots stick to my clothes. As I pick them off, I remind myself that in these dry specks is hidden life, that even as I clear the garden, the seeds for its renewal are there.

Ongoing Clearing

Weekly clearing is part of my garden routine. I sweep away clods of soil and bits and pieces of plant material that have been tracked onto walkways, steps, and decking. The repeated, sweeping motions of the broom allow thoughts to arise. I remind myself to attend to problems while they are small and manageable—like the bits and pieces I sweep from the walk—so they don't build up and obscure my purpose, my path in my life and relationships.

In another act of clearing, I rake leaves and papers blown in by the wind. I take care that the rake doesn't break the stalks of established plants or uproot small, tender seedlings. I work slowly and carefully, since the projecting prongs of my rake, which are there to gather, may also damage. I want the rake to pass over lightly, to take up what I want it to remove, and to smooth the surface—but not to dig in and hurt the plants.

With hand shears I clip grasses and trim dead flowers, branches, and weeds that stray into space belonging to other plants. The art of cutting and clipping is an exact one. I feel a sense of order and control as I remove the excess or the extraneous from my garden.

A friend who is a social worker recently finished a work-study residency as a gardener at a personal growth center on the West Coast. She told me of her experience there: "I was surprised at how strenuous the work was. I had to carry and lift much more than I was used to. But the thing I liked the best was edging borders. I had this certain edging tool and I got pretty good at using it, and I'd move around the garden at a fast clip. It helped me a lot to define and redefine those borders over the months I was there. Each time I dug my tool into the ground and cut back the overgrowth I'd say to myself, 'You're over there and I'm over here.' It helped me to work through my own inability to maintain personal boundaries with my clients who are elderly and ill. It's really difficult for me not to get overly involved and burn out."

It is important for us to attend to ongoing clearing, to prevent one thing from overtaking another, choking it, crowding it out. Attention must be paid.

Couples who come for counseling have first to clear away the residue of past hurts and resentment—a residue that has built up and obscured or obliterated the loving feelings that first brought them together. As they remove these obstacles, they can regain perspective and balance and see again the vital core of their relationship. Then they must learn ways to keep the path of their relationship "swept," to clear feelings as they arise so that there will be no accumulation of rancor, no building of antagonisms.

Clearing for Emotional and Spiritual Balance

Take time now to find a quiet place in which to relax. Close your eyes and bring yourself back to the Mind Garden that you created in Chapter 1. If you gave your Mind Garden a name, you may want to say it to yourself.

Be in your garden. Take a look around. Go over its details, recalling the step-by-step process of creating it, remembering its location, the soil, the way in which you designed it, whether it has paths and fountains, whether it is walled or fenced. Then look at all of the plants, shrubs, trees, borders, and flower beds, and see how they are growing.

Recall the initial clearing you did when you made your Mind Garden. Now take a fresh look to see whether there is any further clearing you need to do. Is something calling your attention that you may have wanted to attend to but didn't? Is there trash or rubble you may have overlooked? Or a stump that still needs to be removed? Take time now and complete this clearing, providing optimum conditions for your garden to flourish.

Is it spring? Do you need to remove the debris of winter so that new growth can reach the sun? Or autumn, when it is necessary to cut back perennials for fuller bloom in spring?

What else needs to be cleared in your garden? Do paths and walkways need sweeping or raking? Have clods of soil and bits of plant material littered the paths? Sweep and rake the debris from your Mind Garden. As you rake and sweep, think of what pathways in your life are blocked and need to be "swept" or "raked." Perhaps you are holding onto some anger or sadness that needs expression, or perhaps a problem from childhood that needs to be recognized and worked out is blocking you from the achievement of a goal.

Are grasses and dead flowers, branches and weeds growing into space belonging to other plants? Are borders in your Mind Garden becoming overgrown? Use an edging tool to tidy borders and push back intruding growth. Use hand shears to trim dead flowers and stems. How does this apply in your own life? Are boundaries becoming unclear? Is work overtaking time needed for solitude or recreation; is it overflowing into time you would like to spend with a loved one? Do you need to cut back, to trim? Think now of what you need to do in your own life for ongoing maintenance.

Complete the clearing of your garden at a relaxed pace, breathing and moving within your own natural rhythm, stopping to rest when you need to. Work in a relaxed and thoughtful manner.

When you have finished, take a few moments to rest. Look around you. Reflect on what you have accomplished and the manner in which you have worked. Were you able to clear in a relaxed manner without exhausting yourself? How do you feel about what you have done?

Now think of ways in which you can hold onto this relaxed and aware state of mind as you resume your daily activities. If, as you proceed through the day, you find yourself feeling rushed or stressed, pause for a moment and take a few deep breaths. Become aware of when you began to lose the natural pace you were able to find while mind gardening and resolve to restore that state of mind. Stand up and stretch or take a short walk. Concentrate on your breathing until you regain your feeling of balance.

Mind gardening is an ongoing process that you can tap into any time you want. Today you were able to assess your clearing needs and to implement them. Return again whenever you like.

RITUAL FOR A SMALL GARDEN

 THIS PAST WINTER was characterized by a seemingly endless thread of gray days. I drew into myself, retreated from the outside world, and rode out the season in a mood of restive discontent.

The coming of spring has sent me to the garden. I want to reconnect with those parts of myself that have been covered over. I want to join in, be part of the rhythm and hum of growth I feel around me.

In this spirit I approach a small neglected corner of my yard that I haven't cultivated before, I feel relieved to be outdoors, in the warm sun with flowers on my mind. My cat Henry sits on the patio watching the birds in the fruit trees.

The soil in this corner of the yard is hard and dry. Dandelions, crabgrass, and oxalis cover the surface. I wet it down and wait a while before I begin to dig.

When was there last a garden here? Aside from some unruly hedges gone awry and a gnarled old rosebush, I find no clue that anyone has ever cared about this small piece of land.

Yet just as I begin to feel solitary, alone even amidst the hum of my garden, I am given a surprise. While digging up weeds and turning the soil, my fingers touch the edges of something hard. I unearth some hand-forged square nails caked with rust and hold them in my palm. I am not the only one to have worked here.

As I continue digging, I discover a white glass marble shot through with orange, a miniature toy car with rubber wheels, an old medicine bottle shining with the colors of the rainbow, and quantities of peach pits. I pile them to one side as I work.

This small collection of remainders is my only link here with people from the past. Remnants of construction and of a fruiting tree, signs of children long ago, they offer an archaeology too sketchy to satisfy.

I imagine my house being built in 1896, and I think about the carpenter who left these nails behind. Did he have a handlebar mustache and wear suspenders? I wonder what elixir the old medicine bottle held and what the peaches that must have grown here tasted like. I conjure images of children playing in this backyard. Where are they now?

I feel a desire to form a bond with this small piece of earth, and with others who plant and grow. Words like *consecrate, sacred, bless* come to mind. But I am not a religious woman. I have no drums, no dance, no paean to the sun. Dressed in jeans, T-shirt, and work boots, I wonder, are these my vestments?

I think back further to a time before houses were here, when indigenous people must have lived on this land. I close my eyes and see a montage of brown faces, shells and beads on earth-smeared bodies, some carrying offerings, others drumming to evoke forces of beneficence at planting time. I hear waves of music and stomping feet, invocations to gods and goddesses of rain and sun, songs of praise and adoration.

I recall a teenage boy, the son of a friend, who had dug a hole in a waterlogged portion of lawn in search of a break in a leaky irrigation pipe—and then had impulsively smeared his face and upper torso with mud. The sight of him seated on the edge of his excavation, a bare-chested, brown-faced blond boy, his eyes white sockets, struck a chord in me. When he saw me looking at him, he arranged himself in a mock-serious pose. I had my camera and photographed him. The moment held an eerie magic, broken by a shriek of his mother as she came unexpectedly on the outlandish scene and yelled at him to "clean up that mess."

Off to the side of my garden plot, in a corner near the fence, I squat and form a small earthen mound, which I shape and smooth with my bare hands. I carefully arrange the peach pits to circle the top and put the marble in the middle. With a cloth, I wipe the caked dirt from the toy car and the bottle and set them on either side of the mound. Then I lay the square nails end to end around its base.

Having arranged my relics in this way satisfies something deep within. I've made my own communion with the spirits that inhabit this place. Now, we are all here.

I sprinkle purple and white alyssum seeds on the mound, water them, and begin to plant my garden.

3

DIGGING

*. . . to dig deep into the actual
and get something out of that—
this doubtless is the right way to live.*

HENRY JAMES

WHO AMONG US CANNOT remember kneeling, shovel in hand, while digging in the dirt? What matter whether rocks or pebbles scratched us, whether clothes, shoes, or hands were muddied? What matter if we were scolded for getting dirty and had later to endure being stripped and scrubbed?

Digging was the natural thing to do. We were close to the earth, and it was second nature to investigate its vastness and variety, whether in a country field, backyard, vacant city lot, or on a sandy beach.

It seemed there was nothing we couldn't do with the earth.

When shovels and pails were lost or broken, we'd use sticks, spoons, and even our hands to scoop, mound, and mold.

Sometimes we dug just to see what we'd find. The moisture and grit of the dirt, its earthy, pungent smell, the mystery of it lured us. We'd look for buried treasure and find earthworms, sow bugs, pieces of oxidized glass, rusty nails. Once in a while we'd strike gold—an encrusted Indianhead penny or buffalo nickel. A sense of adventure and a belief that we could do anything spurred us on.

Through gardening we can reexperience this close connection to the earth. As adults we still feel the pleasure and excitement of childhood as we are drawn to seek what is beneath the soil, but as gardeners, our search has more purpose. Long-handled spading forks and trowels replace the sticks, pails, and tiny shovels of childhood.

We now dig to investigate the nature and condition of the soil and to prepare it for planting. Each new garden is a set of unknowns to be explored and understood. Despite our enthusiasm to plant, we must be patient and first take care of fundamental soil needs. None of our efforts will bear fruit if the soil is not properly evaluated and prepared. The soil is the foundation of the garden.

Digging to Evaluate the Soil

It is a clear day in early April. The warm sun of a cloudless morning makes this a perfect day to turn the soil for my new garden. I'm eager to begin; I have already waited a week for the earth to dry after a heavy spring rain.

I scoop some soil into my hand and crumble it between my fingers. It's moist and breaks up easily, like good loam. But this is only the topsoil. Has someone planted here before? I don't know what lies beneath the surface. Which of the three basic soil types do I have—clay, sand, or loam?

The first thrusts of my spading fork turn up large clods of heavy soil. It's airless, thick, and moist. I see that it's clay, which, although rich in nutrients, doesn't drain well. Wet and dark, it reminds me of the dirt I made mud pies with when I was a child.

Some kinds of native plants might thrive in this dense soil. Such plants have learned to store water in roots that spread along the surface. But the roots of the plants I'm going to use will need to grow deep and will be unable to penetrate this thick earth. I'll have to improve the soil before I plant.

The same would be true if I found my garden soil to be sandy. I'll know it's sandy if it runs through my fingers. Although porous and easier to dig than clay, water percolates through sandy soil, taking with it the nutrients vital for plant growth. Dry and lightweight, sandy soil is easily eroded by the wind.

Garden plants that grow in sandy soil will have to struggle to survive. Their roots will need to seek far below the surface for water and food. Above ground, malnourished stems and leaves will suffer the drying effects of wind and sun.

Loam, the ideal garden soil, lies midway between the two extremes and provides the best environment for garden plants. It isn't hard to recognize. It's the "peaty," somewhat moist, easy-to-crumble soil we find in nursery beds and botanical gardens and in the potted plants we purchase.

Made up of two-thirds clay, fine rock, and sand and of one-third animal and vegetable matter, it's sandy enough to drain well but has enough clay to hold reserves of water and food. Yet its open texture makes it easy to work. In it my plants can root firmly and reach the water, air, and nutrients they need in order to flourish.

On this clear April day I've discovered that my soil is dense clay. You may come across clay, sandy soil, or loam as you dig your garden. Join me now as I prepare my garden soil for planting so that you'll know what to do when you prepare yours.

Preparing the Garden Soil

First I need to break up and aerate this heavy soil.

I work steadily, turning the earth with my long spading fork, then spearing the heavy clods, opening them to the air.

I sink the fork into the tightly packed earth, digging and turning it two spades deep. Although the soil is heavy and I can feel my muscles strain as I dig, I persevere. If I want my plants to be deep rooted and safe in drought and flood, I must prepare the soil to a depth of two feet below the surface.

When I've finished breaking up the clods, I add a mixture of humus and compost, working it down through the overturned earth until the soil is lighter and more open. As it becomes softer and more friable, I take pleasure in turning the rich, dark earth.

The amendments I've added and further exposure to the air and sun cause the clods to break into smaller "crumbs," which give the soil a more airy, open structure. Now the texture is what it should be—sandy enough to drain well but with enough clay to hold essential reserves. The soil is medium to dark brown in color, weighs less than clay but more than sandy soil, crumbles easily, is slightly moist, and contains particles of sand, clay, and humus (or whatever other organic amendments I've used).

The "recipe" for making loam from sandy soil is the same as that for amending clay: Add organic amendments such as compost, leaf mold, wood shavings, and manure until the soil drains well but still holds water and nutrients.

You can test the soil by wetting it down and watching to see how the water flows through it. If it has too much clay, the water will sit on the surface for a while. If it has too much sand, the water will be sucked in too rapidly, leaving the surface area dry. If it's loam, the water will dampen all of the soil evenly.

I think about clay, sand, and loam as I dig, of how they resemble certain human character types. I play with this idea in my mind.

"Clay" types are people who are hard to get through to, retentive and withholding. Like a layer of clay, they hold onto resources. They take in slowly and don't let go easily. Relating to them requires effort on our part, like digging up clay soil. They tend to be stoic and uncommunicative.

Walter is a "clay" type of person. He thinks for a very long time before he makes a decision and can't decide simple things like which restaurant or movie to go to. His ponderous manner and lack of spontaneity take the adventure and joy out of the most casual activity. This makes life difficult for friends and family who think of him as a "stick-in-the-mud" and avoid socializing with him.

"Sandy" types are just the opposite. They have poorly defined boundaries and a poorly developed sense of themselves. They are too forthcoming and can't absorb and hold onto their self-worth. They are constantly seeking approval and love from others. Like sandy soil, they tend to "wash out," squandering their resources. These types of people tend to be scattered in their approach to life and often have difficulty feeling fulfilled.

I think of Sara as this type of person. The course of her life is determined by the actual or perceived needs of friends and family. She is focused on pleasing others and spends at least half of her day on the telephone listening to the problems of her friends and the other half running errands and performing chores for her family.

She has few interests of her own and wonders why she is so nervous. Periodically she reaches a point where she has exhausted all of her resources, and then she explodes hysterically, screaming at her husband and children.

"Loam" types, like the best garden soil, have more balanced temperaments. They are open and receptive, able to support and nourish life around them, yet able to maintain their own integrity.

Paula is a working single mother, responsible for two teenagers and her aging widowed mother. While she is caring and nurturing, she is also aware of her own need for time apart from the family. She makes time regularly to pursue her interest in nature photography.

When her mother and children ask more of her time and energy than she is capable of giving, she is able to refuse them without guilt. She knows that as the single head of a household, she must maintain a balanced emotional soil.

We want a fertile and balanced soil in which to grow our goals, relationships, and work. We want our ideas and plans to take firm root. Otherwise, they will fall victim to the unexpected stresses of life.

Digging to Renew, Replenish, and Repair

In additon to digging to make a new garden, we must also dig periodically to renew and replenish the soil.

Even the best of soils needs renewal and replenishment. Rain and melting snow close up the air spaces between soil particles until water can no longer flow through easily. Over time, the pressure of foot traffic causes further soil consolidation and depletion of the oxygen essential for plant growth. To open up space between soil particles, I must periodically aerate my garden soil so that water and plant nutrients can reach the roots.

With time, my garden soil also becomes depleted of essential nutrients. Organic materials in the earth are continuously being broken down by tiny organisms in the soil. Nitrogen, phosphorus, potassium, and other nutrients are consumed in this process. These elements are vital to the growth of my plants, and I must replace them, adding amendments such as humus, leaf mold, wood shavings, and manure, working them at least six inches deep into the soil with my shovel.

Many people, even those gifted with natural vigor and energy, fail to realize when their resources are being depleted. Even though you may be in good health, it is important that you routinely replenish and renew your own emotional and physical reserves.

The need to replace depleted resources is a natural one. Just as we need to sleep each night, we need to take time on a regular basis to relax with a good book, walk along the ocean or a quiet woodland stream, and enjoy ourselves with friends and family.

If you find yourself experiencing repeated illness or if you're forgetting things more than usual or are frequently out of sorts, it's time to take stock of your resources. In time of stress, you may need extra replenishment. This may be particularly true if you have neglected for some time the ongoing need to renew your physical and emotional reserves.

These oversights are most likely to occur when people lead "surface" or superficial lives and ignore the condition of their emotional "subsoil." They don't see digging as an integral part of maintaining good health, so they live only in their "topsoil." They do not make the time to assess and consider their inner lives, to examine their relationships, to see what underlies their attitudes, motives, and behaviors.

It is only when their life garden fails to thrive, when they experience disaster and failure, that they are willing to consider the need to dig deeper and probe the "subsoil" of their emotional lives.

John, a computer engineer, reluctantly came to see me with his wife Barbara, a teacher. He sat silently, his face expressionless, as she tearfully spoke of her loneliness and frustration. "Although John has always been a good provider and I know deep down he cares for me, I might as well be alone. We rarely have a conversation, and he never tells me how he feels about anything."

She went on to say that although they had been married for fifteen years, she felt she really didn't know him, that if he was unhappy or if they had a disagreement, he would leave or withdraw into himself. When decisions that involved the two of them needed to be made, he would not volunteer his preferences and usually, by default, deferred to her. "I'm tired of feeling like a nag. I love you, John, but if things don't change I'm going to leave."

When John heard this last remark, he leaned forward in his chair and spoke, "I've never been able to express my feelings. I'm willing to change—I just don't know how to do it. I don't want to lose you."

I've heard variations of this dialogue between couples many, many times. Although not always gender specific, the themes are most often divided along the lines of societally proscribed sex roles. The women express a longing for closeness, conversation, and intimacy, which is more than sexual. The men, unable to express themselves at a deep emotional level, able to maneuver quite well in the areas of logic, business, and sports, but living as marginal figures in their marriages and families, existing on the peripheries of emotional life.

Many of these men lead alienating and lonely lives. They separate and divorce for reasons that are remediable, and they fall prey to stress-related diseases.

Several years ago I decided to form a group to help men reconnect with their repressed emotions and learn skills for expression.

I invited John to join this group. As he heard the other men speak, he became aware of how similar his story was to theirs, how because of societal prohibitions, he had covered over layers of deeper emotions and trained himself to live in the superficial "topsoil" of his feelings.

He, like the other men, spent much of his time in group digging to the source of his inability to feel and to convey what he felt. Feelings of pain, rejection, and ridicule were haltingly expressed as John unearthed his past.

He remembered being called a "sissy" by another boy when he was five and had cried after falling from a playground swing. He recalled, too, a disdainful remark of his father's that he was acting "like a girl" when John, at age eight, clutched at his father during a frightening scene in a horror movie.

The dense emotional armor he had gradually affected worked well for him in the world of men but was a disaster for his marriage. Fortunately, as John dug to the subsoil of his emotional life, reexperiencing the pain and losses of childhood, he was able to reclaim a part of himself and to learn how to talk about his feelings—first, in the safe environment of the group and then, later, with Barbara.

Like John, a lot of people don't dig until they have to—until they have a problem. We mustn't only dig at a point of crisis to remedy a problem that's already been produced. It's important to dig periodically to renew and replenish—and to keep smaller problems from growing into larger ones.

When Not to Dig

We can't always be digging. We need to allow time for the garden to progress through its natural cycle. You don't want to unearth seeds before they germinate or to damage the roots of tender plants. You must learn to trust the garden's own evolution, to guard and protect it but never tamper with it. The garden has a life of its own. In planting your garden, you're setting in motion a process with its own momentum and life energy. You, the gardener, may create favorable conditions for growth by properly preparing the soil, but you can only be a witness to the evolution of the garden.

In the same way, you can't always be analyzing and working on yourself. You can't be in control of everything. You need to pace yourself and recognize that things will take care of themselves in time, that plans and dreams need to evolve and mature, and that overzealousness may uproot them prematurely.

If you spend too much time digging down into yourself, you'll miss out on what's really happening at the moment, and life will pass you by. The purpose of digging is to begin a natural process. It's not an end in itself.

Louise, a woman in her thirties, was referred to me by a therapist who was leaving the area. An only child, Louise was born when her parents were in their forties. She was described to me as intelligent but socially isolated. She'd been in therapy for over six years.

Although Louise wept over her loneliness and expressed a longing for close relationships, she seemed less interested in finding a solution to her problem than in analyzing the cause of her dilemma. I wondered what she had been doing in her past six years of therapy!

She was at a loss to suggest ways she could begin to take steps to break out of her isolation and was resistant to any tentative suggestions about how she might begin to make contact with others. At each offering, she would respond with a "yes, but" and then go back over her past history analyzing why she was the way she was and why she couldn't take any steps toward change. She was interested only in the "why" of things and not in the "how to."

It was clear to me that Louise would have to stop her obsessive digging and move on to planting seeds for behaviors likely to increase her opportunities for social contact. I was concerned that since digging had become her main occupation and served her well as a defense against fear and imagined rejection, she would be unwilling to give it up.

Sadly, this was the case. I made the completion of weekly behavioral assignments a condition for continuing to work with her. She made only halfhearted efforts to do them, and I suggested that she stop coming to see me for a while and think through what she was willing to do to have her situation improve.

Louise called a few weeks later to say that she could see what I meant but that she wasn't ready to do more. She discontinued her therapy with me.

Just as digging and redigging the garden can be nonproductive, so we may find that digging in soil that is inhospitable for planting may be fruitless.

In your garden you may encounter hardpan, an impervious layer of soil at or near the surface that will not yield to shovel or spading fork. Hardpan occurs either as a natural formation, usually in the Southwest, or elsewhere as a human-made condition, developing at building sites as heavy equipment passes back and forth over excavated subsoil.

Roots can't penetrate hardpan, and water can't drain through it. In order to pierce hardpan, you have to plow or drill.

Isn't that the way it happens in life? We encounter hardpan sometimes. We have work, living conditions, or relationships that just don't work no matter how hard we try. We've told ourselves what we need to do in these situations, but our jobs, our living situations, or intimate relationships don't respond to our efforts.

We have to ask ourselves whether we should be gardening elsewhere. We need to recognize when conditions are inhospitable and give ourselves permission to move on.

It may be a wise choice to decide against a garden where you encounter hardpan. You need to assess your resources and see whether it would be better to make a garden somewhere else.

Digging for Emotional and Spiritual Balance

To do your emotional digging, you need to relax. Find a quiet space and get into a comfortable position. Close your eyes, take some deep breaths, and relax the muscle groups in your body one by one. Continue to focus on your breathing while you bring yourself to your Mind Garden.

Once you've arrived, look around you. Go over the details of your garden, remembering all that you did to create it. Recall its location, overall design, and such things as walkways, benches, and fences. Let your eyes follow the contours of trees, the colors of flowers, the size of plants. Take a look and see how they are growing.

Recall the digging you did when you made your Mind Garden.

Look to see whether there is any further digging you wish to do. Are any plants drooping, stunted, or spindly even though you've fed and watered them and checked for pests and disease?

Is the garden you envisioned failing to thrive? Are plants tall and leggy or short and shallow-rooted? Are they struggling to find sustenance in the soil?

Don't worry if things are not working according to plan. Although when you conceived it your vision was a perfect one for you, you may not have known how to bring this plan to fruition as you proceeded to make your garden.

This happens all of the time in life. We encounter problems as we attempt to transform our dreams into reality. Often we abandon them at these times of difficulty.

Through understanding garden processes, we will gradually be able to align our visions and dreams with the realities we encounter in life and in the garden.

As we come to see that the obstacles we encounter in our gardens and in our lives are natural occurrences and not bad luck, we can use them as opportunities through which we can learn and grow.

Perhaps you didn't spend enough time preparing the soil when you first made your Mind Garden. Maybe you didn't know how to evaluate it to see whether it was clay, sand, or loam. Or perhaps you began to aerate and amend the soil but found it too strenuous and decided not to improve it. Now that you see the problem, you want to correct it.

There are many ways to garden. You have your own rhythm, your own pace, your own unique way. You may not want to dig your garden all at once. Know your own limits. You may wish to break the digging into manageable segments and then do the same when you add the amendments. Tending your Mind Garden will help you discover the best way for you to pace yourself. Mistakes there can be corrected. You can redig your garden.

Spend time now adding leaf mold, compost, or manure to your garden soil, improving the structure so that water, air, and nutrients can find their way to plant roots and then drain easily. You may lose some of your garden plants in this process, but the new ones you plant will have a better chance for survival.

Perhaps it's spring, and though your garden plants are growing well, the garden soil needs its periodic replenishment. Take time to turn the soil and mix in necessary amendments such as leaf mold, manure, and humus so that new plants will find rich, well-aerated soil to root in.

To avoid stagnation and depletion of our own mental and physical resources, we must replenish and renew them. Eating well, getting enough rest, and making time for recreation and education will provide the variety and enrichment necessary for balance and stability.

Digging need not be all sweat and muscle. The repeated rhythm of the thrusting, lifting, and turning you do with your shovel or spading fork can also be relaxing. Even more, the knowledge that you are freeing the soil to breathe and enhancing its ability to nurture what you have planted can be deeply satisfying.

When you have finished digging, put your shovel or spading fork aside and rest. Look around you and see what you have accomplished. Were you able to pace yourself as you dug? How do you feel about the digging you have done?

Were you able to complete what you set out to do during this visit to your Mind Garden? If you weren't able to finish digging, remember that you can return at any time to renew, replenish, or repair.

MAKING MY WAY TO THE GARDEN

We shall not cease from exploration

And the end of all our exploring

Will be to arrive where we started

And know the place for the first time.

T. S. ELIOT

 BEFORE I KNEW what gardening was, I was a gardener. I was instinctively drawn to the colors, smells, sounds, and textures of Nature. My earliest memories are of finding violets and jack-in-the-pulpits on the tree-shaded banks of a stream that ran through Bronx River Park. Around age four or five, I remember sitting on an expanse of green grass staring at a clump of bright yellow dandelions. The warmth of the sun on my shoulders, my bare thighs damp from the clover-scented grass—it seemed there was nothing between me and the flowers: In one perfect moment we had merged and become one.

I was fascinated with the way small plants grew through the cracks in sidewalk pavement and how daffodils and jonquils pushed up through melting snow. In March when leaf buds opened on barren branches, confirming that trees I thought must surely be frost dead were alive, a worried vigilance within me relaxed.

Inside the house I kept an eye on the Chinese evergreen that grew in a crystal pitcher on the dining room table. I could see the whole plant, the dark green heart-shaped leaves above a thick, horizontally striped stem, the long, coiled roots that sat in slimy, stagnant water which filled the vase. How did it grow, I wondered?

My love of plants seemed to be a private fascination.

I'd never seen anyone in my family plant anything. In a time before penicillin, when polio, measles, and tuberculosis were still common, the soil was associated with germs and disease, and putting one's hands in dirt was discouraged. My interest in growing things was tolerated but not encouraged, and the spark within me found no outlet.

But even without nurturance, my attachment to Nature grew.

Each weekday I walked six blocks to and from P.S. 80, across Jerome Avenue and under the elevated train. Some days it was my misfortune to cross this street as a train passed overhead. I'd find myself caught up in a cyclonic aftermath in which the street litter of newspapers and cigarette butts and candy wrappers was stirred into dust devils. I'd clutch my skirt while trying futilely to shield my eyes and nostrils from the flying dirt. Each of these assaults infuriated me. I longed to find a way to clean up the world and make it beautiful.

It wasn't until much later in life that I was able to see that these strong, persistent feelings about Nature and my longing for beauty were, in reality, an intuitive voice urging me toward the garden.

This inner voice, the one that speaks to us in the language of our first and deepest desires, is never truly lost. As I bring my flower beds to bloom and my young trees to flower and fruit, as I make a garden world within three backyard fences, I reunite with that young girl who hungered for beauty. I can feel her now, within me, calmer, more satisfied.

Each of us will hear a different voice, one that is unique to us, and we will each be called in a different direction. But once heard, we must find the courage to reunite with that voice and trust where it leads. It is the voice of our truest nature. If we fail to heed its inner call, we will be less than we might have been, and we will never truly find peace and a sense of completeness.

4

PLANTING

Whether you tend a garden or not,
you are the gardener of your own
being, the seed of your destiny.

THE FINDHORN COMMUNITY

P

LANTING A GARDEN IS AN act of optimism. When you plant a seed, you put hope in the ground. Your trust is in the future when there is no present sign that life will come.

After the spare servings of color that winter gives, we yearn to break that long gray fast. Warm sun coaxes bloom from branch and green-sheathed buds open into rousing shades of coral, pink, and yellow. Our eyes feast on early flowering redbud, acacia, and quince, which flamingly announce themselves against a muted backdrop of dormant earth.

We feel within us a particular stirring that echoes the stirring in the land around us. We, too, can bring life to the garden.

Preparing for Planting

I wait for a calm, windless morning when the danger of frost has past and visit the local nursery where I shop for seeds, bulbs, and seedlings. Although mine is a California garden and I can plant throughout the year, there is no time like spring for awakening the gardener in me.

I'm delighted by the array of fresh young plants both familiar and new: tender poppy and viola seedlings planted six to a tray, bins and boxes of summer-flowering lilies, giant dahlias and gladiolus, seed packets with brightly colored pictures, pots of orchids and ferns.

I've already put in my roses and fruit trees, so I pass these by. In January, during bare-root season when deciduous trees and shrubs are dormant, I planted two different kinds of roses: a climbing pink Queen Elizabeth along the picket fence and a white Jack Frost in the rose bed. I also planted an apricot and a coastal fig tree.

The bare-root roses, the apricot, and the fig looked like lifeless twigs when I bought them. But planting them while they were still dormant gave them an advantage. They had a chance to develop strong roots and establish themselves in their growing space before they needed to use their energies to produce leaves and flowers. The ones I see here at the nursery crowded into plastic containers are small and root bound, while mine are twice the size, flourishing vigorously in rich garden loam.

I'm tempted to add a new variety of rhododendron to my already ample collection, but I resist the urge. I remove the container from my cart and return it to its shelf. Once I planted too many ferns in a small shade garden, and none of them did well. I learned that a decision not to do something in the garden is as important as a decision to do something.

Inexperienced gardeners often buy too many plants, which they then cram haphazardly into their backyards. If planted too close to one another, these seedlings will have to compete for water and nutrients and won't reach their full growth, if they survive at all. Air can't circulate freely between crowded plants, and they become breeding places for harmful insects and diseases.

As I make the rest of my selections, I remind myself that I am not only introducing an individual begonia, camellia, or marguerite but a plant that will be part of this particular community of growing things I am creating. My choices must be made with the whole garden environment in mind.

The art of gardening lies in understanding the needs of each flower, shrub, or tree we introduce and in integrating it into the overall garden design. We want each plant to grow strong and healthy and at the same time to live in harmony with the others.

When I've unloaded my containers from the car and carried them into the garden, I glance at the yard and take stock of what is already there.

A tall privet hedge runs along a fence on the southern boundary of my property. In front of it grows a lush stand of white calla lilies. It's a perfect spot for a shade garden. I started one there last year.

In a sunny place near the kitchen window, I've dug and prepared a bed of fine loam where I'll plant some summer-flowering marigolds and zinnia seeds. I like to watch the progress of my seedlings from a window near the breakfast table.

Along a west wall is a large freshly dug bed where I've cleared away some camellias and cinerarias that had been badly burned by the sun. These shade-loving plants were mistakenly planted in a sunny location by someone who gardened here before I came.

In the same bed, I've left a gardenia that has, thus far, refused to bloom. It, too, was here when I came. Gardenias need heat to flower. They're not suited to the relatively cool summers of my Central California location. Since the plant itself appears healthy, I'll give it another season in the garden to see if it blooms.

Knowing the light requirements of my plants is important. Shade-loving plants will burn up and die in the sun, and sun-loving ones won't flower in the shade. The more we deviate from providing the proper light and temperature for our plants, the greater the chance we take that they won't survive.

As I carry my plants into the garden, I make a mental note of where they'll go: ferns and fuchsia in the shade, pansies, lobelia, alyssum, and poppies in the sun, Canterbury bells and foxglove in a partially shaded spot. I then group them in the areas where they'll go.

Planting

To the shade garden I add a delicate maidenhair fern and a pink and purple fuchsia already in bud. With a trowel I dig two planting holes under a tall Australian tree fern.

I tilt the pots that hold the maidenhair fern and fuchsia, tap their bottoms to loosen the roots, and carefully remove the plants. I do this slowly and gently; if the root ball breaks, the plant may die.

In the holes I've dug under the tree fern's broad fronds, I gently set the plants. I sprinkle soil into the empty spaces around the roots, filling in the holes to the soil line and then tamping the earth firmly. Then I scoop out some of the surface dirt to form a small, saucerlike depression that will serve as a reservoir for water.

Next, in front of the ferns and fuchsias, I set in a border of pink fairy primroses. The seedlings, which have been planted six to a tray, are small and their roots are fragile. I make sure that the soil is moist so that it will not fall away from the roots as I dislodge the seedlings from the tray. I place each primrose in its planting hole and tamp the soil. Then I fill my watering can and wet down all of the things I've planted with water mixed with vitamin B_1 to lessen the shock of transplanting.

The importance of exercising extreme care with new young things cannot be emphasized enough. Hasty or rough handling during planting may cause root, stem, or leaf breakage. Failure to water or prevent transplant shock may injure or kill the plants, causing all of our efforts to be for naught.

The same can be said of any beginning we make. We must be aware that in starting a new enterprise or relationship we will undergo the stresses of adaptation and change.

It's important to pay attention, act thoughtfully, and find ways to nurture and support these beginnings.

We often underestimate the special stresses of new beginnings. I remember starting a job as a program director in a shelter for abused and abandoned children. In addition to the demanding schedule of meetings with children, social workers, and psychiatrists, I had to set up the office, establish rapport with the staff, and create and maintain a stable and caring environment for the children themselves. For the first several months, I found I was working ten- or twelve-hour days, dealing with crisis after crisis, rarely even stopping for lunch. I had to take extra care during this transition time to get enough sleep, to work in my garden, and to stay in close touch with friends.

Starting a job, dealing with the arrival of a new baby, adjusting to a new relationship are events that require care, attention, empathy. This attitude of care and nurturance is critical. We don't want to do anything roughly or haphazardly just to get it done.

In my garden, I now move to the seed bed and read the planting directions on the seed packets of marigolds and zinnias. Running the point of my trowel over the soil's surface, I create two long, shallow rows, one for each kind of seed.

I place each seed in the ground, following the planting instructions for proper spacing and depth. Then I cover them with soil, which I pat down with my hands, and sprinkle the earth with water, being careful not to wash the seeds away.

When I've finished putting in the shade plants and seeds, I move to the wide, newly dug plot I've prepared along a sunny west wall. Here I'll set some annuals for summer color. In the rear, against the wall, I plant a row of blue delphiniums, the tallest of the flowers. Even though they look small now, they will grow to about three feet, so I space them eighteen inches apart, leaving room for them to spread. I put a wooden stake in the soil behind each seedling. As the plants mature, I'll tie them to the stakes for support.

In the next row, I put in medium-sized snapdragons in pinks and purples, alternated, for variety, with dusty miller, which will grow to the same height. In front of these, I finish my planting with a border of low-growing blue violas.

Most of the things I've added to the garden are annuals, plants like snapdragons and pansies that last for just one season and then must be grown again from seed.

It's the foundation plants and perennials, those shrubs, trees, bulbs, and flowers that last for many years, that give permanence and definition to the garden design.

The gradation of shrubs and perennials, as well as the arrangement of annuals we add each season, is an aesthetic consideration. I arrange my garden with an eye to each plant's size, shape, texture, and color. With some practice and experience, you will be able to envision the patterns plants will make and to use your knowledge to realize your own unique plan, much as an artist uses a palette to create a picture or as a composer orchestrates all the instruments to complete a symphony. A garden can be a work of art.

The aesthetics of smell and sound can be expressed as well by including plantings of aromatic flowers, trees, and shrubs and by incorporating the sounds of running water and the rustle of leaves into the total sensory experience of the garden.

Even though I've selected and arranged the colors and shapes of my flowers to suit my tastes, I leave room for the unexpected. No matter how carefully I plan, there are always chance occurrences that can be serendipitous. Last spring, among the perennials and annuals I planted, some California native poppy seeds volunteered themselves. Interspersed with tall purple iris and pink penstemon was a carpet of orange, a gift from the wind.

I'm feeling a bit stiff, so I stop to rest. I survey my newly planted flower bed and see that it looks rather sparse. I resist the temptation to crowd in more seedlings. Just as I had to refrain from buying too many plants when I shopped in the lush nursery, I have to hold back from planting too much. I remind myself that in a very short time the seeds and plants will take hold and fill in the bare spots.

As I view the small seedlings in their large bed of soil, I think of Ellen who came to me for consultation because she felt she was experiencing writer's block. We soon discovered her problem wasn't that she couldn't complete a story or poem. In her fear and anxiety about starting late in life and not being good enough, Ellen had "planted" too many projects and was attempting to put them into action all at once.

Her expectations of herself were unrealistic, and her mind was a garden overcrowded with seedlings in which nothing was doing well. There wasn't enough room or time for anything to root and take shape adequately.

Through our meetings over the next few months, she was able to see that her projects were like seedlings in the overplanted flower bed of an eager but inexperienced gardener. They were too close to one another, had no breathing space, and were crowding one another out.

We replanted the seeds of her projects one at a time, leaving enough space between them for each to develop healthily. Ellen picked one uncompleted story to work on first. As she experienced problems with scheduling her time, expecting too much of herself, or fearing she was too old to succeed at writing, we discussed and resolved them one at a time.

Within two months Ellen had completed one of her stories to her satisfaction and had begun to build a sense of confidence in her work and an understanding of how to pace herself. In the following months, as we repeated this process, she was able to complete several more stories and poems.

Although she experiences the doubts and fears common to most writers, Ellen now works regularly on her poems and stories. She consults with me from time to time when she begins to slip into old patterns of planting too many projects at once and when she needs to sort things out.

Our gardens, for better or worse, reflect who we are. The way you approach your garden can tell you a lot about the way you approach life. People who start projects but don't finish them will probably do the same in their gardens. They'll plant more than they can tend and come to see the garden as an endless series of chores. Eventually they'll abandon it.

In life we can see ourselves putting too many plans into action, unable or unwilling to make choices. Although we may experience ourselves working very hard to succeed, we aren't able to devote the attention required to each enterprise, and we end up not doing anything really well. We feel a sense of despair and depression and blame ourselves for failure.

The garden teaches us that it is the process, not the product, that matters. You don't have to produce the biggest or the best in your garden. Your garden is just for you. Feel free to find your own pace and pleasure there, being careful not to replicate patterns demanded of you in the work world. Gardening should not be a competition but a time for reconnecting with yourself.

Planting for Emotional and Spiritual Balance

It's time now for you to pause and find a quiet place in which to relax. Close your eyes, breathe deeply, and as you've done before, relax the muscle groups throughout your body one at a time. As you breathe and relax, return to your Mind Garden.

Visualize your own plans and projects as you look around you. Think of how they parallel what you see as you take stock of the trees, shrubs, and flowers that are already there. Are they just beginning to set buds in early spring? Are they beginning to leaf out in April or May? Do they have enough space and light?

What areas of the garden are barren? Are there places where annuals that flowered and gave pleasure for a season have finished their bloom? Are there new planting beds ready to receive flowers and shrubs? Or perhaps you notice a flower or shrub that has failed to survive and that you'd like to replace.

Not everything we plant grows. Some plants, like some plans and relationships, fail to take root and survive. These failures may occur because the seeds or seedlings themselves were defective. In this case, we can replace them with healthy ones.

In other instances, our plants die because we lacked understanding of the proper way to plant or because we didn't know the growing requirements of a particular tree, shrub, or flower.

We mustn't be discouraged by our initial losses in the garden. They may make us feel sad, but if we identify the reason a plant failed, we can increase the chances that the one we plant next time will survive. In the garden, as in life, we become wise and experienced through trial and error.

As you survey your Mind Garden, think about the planting you'd like to do—whether you want to grow annuals or perennials, seeds or seedlings. Perhaps you'd like to try some new flowers, trees, or shrubs, or maybe you'd like to include old favorites.

When you've assembled your plants, think about where you will put them. Think about their needs for shade or sun, the space you'll need to provide between the different seedlings, the color combinations of the flowers, and how tall each will grow, and then arrange the planting beds and borders with these considerations in mind. Take time and care as you remove each one from its container, gently placing it in the ground and covering its roots, then tamping the soil around it.

Next, after reading the directions on the packets, plant your seeds in the beds you've dug for them considering, as you've done with your seedlings, their special needs.

Stop now to rest and enjoy the plantings in your Mind Garden. The harmonious integration of your ideas and the care and attention you have given your garden will, in a short time, bring you much joy and happiness.

AFTERTHOUGHTS

 THIS MORNING I worked in the garden. I trimmed some of the clarkia that was leaning every which way and dwarfing the other flowers. Its tall slender stalks were dotted with rosettes of every shade of pink from pale salmon to deep fuschia, along with the lavender viscaria and blue nigella, and had been the showpieces of my summer garden.

I gave the cut flowers to Pam, who'd given me the seeds. She's reopened her flower stand down the street. We laughed about the "bread cast on the waters" as she put the last of my clarkia on display.

I had almost thrown the seeds away. Pam gave them to me about nine months ago, along with the viscaria and nigella, shortly after I'd moved in. At the time, my garden was hardly a flower or shrub.

It was late winter, and I was working steadily to make a home out of the shambles of a house I'd just purchased. Each day I scrubbed, scraped, and painted the interior, trying to make a place where I could live and work. I was bone-weary and couldn't begin to think of planting seeds. In fact, I lost the little plastic bags of seeds that Pam had placed in my hands.

It wasn't until April, when I finally got rid of the last of the construction mess, that the bags turned up in a pile of old wood and plaster. The labels had fallen off—not that it mattered, for I'd never grown any of the seeds before and couldn't have told one from another. By then I'd planted my spring garden. Icelandic poppies, English daisies, alyssum, foxglove, and iris were already in bloom. I thought of throwing the seeds away but just couldn't bring myself to.

Instead, I matter-of-factly scattered them over the soil.

Again I forgot about them. When their green shoots first appeared among the weeds, I even pulled some out before I remembered what they were. They grew in great abundance around the mature spring flowers, and I didn't bother to thin or transplant them.

The spring flowers have long since gone, but the seeds I so casually planted not only introduced me to three new and charming flowers but also provided most of the garden color from mid-June to mid-July.

How often I've done this in my life: missed opportunities, lost important things and people, thrown them away or forgotten them in a pile of emotional trash. Sometimes the loss is permanent. But sometimes they spring to life again, when I have grown to meet them or when chance or accident tosses them in front of me and magically offers me a second chance, an opportunity to rediscover them.

5

GROWING

Everything is gestation and then birthing.

RAINER MARIA RILKE

ONE OF THE MOST SATISFY-
ing times in the garden comes after I've finished planting,
when I've raked and smoothed the soil around plants and
seed furrows, swept the loose dirt from walkways, stored the
planting containers in the shed, and put away gardening
tools.

When I've scrubbed the dirt from my fingernails and
scraped the mud from my boots, I feel the quiet pleasure of
having completed a large job. This feeling grows as I give
the garden a final wetting down.

A benediction of sorts, I think to myself, as I turn the
fine spray of the hose first to one and then another of my
community of plants. As I move among them, I reflect on
each new plant, what it is now, what I felt when planting it,
what I know of its nature, needs, and potential, and I
silently wish each one well as it begins its journey through
the growing year.

Later, as I sit on my garden bench looking over my
newly planted garden, I find myself having some small mis-
givings. How will everything combine? Did I plant the
young apricot tree too close to the deck? Will the red be-
gonias clash with the coral primroses when they bloom? Is
my overall garden plan too ambitious for my growing
space?

We can never know these things for certain. How close
our vision is to the way things actually turn out is determined partly by how experienced we are and partly by

chance, the mystery of growth, and the intangibles of creative imagining.

I make peace with my doubts and tell myself that all will work out in the end. I reassure myself that in planting my garden, I've set in motion a process in which there will be room for movement and change.

This is a time for seeds and seedlings to settle in and for me to rest and take in what I've done thus far. After the physical activity of clearing, digging, planning, and planting, I want time to relax, to feel the deep satisfaction that comes after the effort exerted to create something new.

Germinating

Along with my sense of gratification, I also feel excited and expectant as I wait for my seeds to grow and my seedlings to take root.

As a child, I remember being unable to wait for the nasturtium seeds I planted to germinate. Curious and impatient, convinced that there must be something wrong with them, I dug them up prematurely.

Below the earth's surface, I uncovered several long white tendrils topped by tiny pale green leaves just forming. I remember holding these slender stems in the palm of my hand. The newly germinated sprouts were still attached to the seed pods from which they were uncoiling. I can still recall my feeling of horror when I realized that I had killed the seeds because I couldn't wait. Left undisturbed, they would have sprouted in a day or two.

As adults we can kill our own hopes and dreams in much the same way impatient children do if we don't see that each plan or idea has its own germinating time. If we fail to recognize this, we may mistakenly dismiss new ideas as silly, or unimportant, or unlikely to succeed—before they even have a chance to form.

Some of us carry this pattern of impatient, premature uprooting into adulthood, moving from one seed of an idea or relationship to another, never allowing these seeds time to germinate and take root.

We all know of a talented relative or friend who hasn't made the most of his or her potential, someone who has never stayed with anything for long or who, in spite of having all of the qualities necessary for success, has failed in life. Often these people lack patience—the ability to wait and to understand that new seeds, whether in relationships or work, need time to develop.

All things of lasting value—a career or profession, the shaping of a creative life or of a solid relationship—take time. But "modern conveniences" such as fast food, instant coffee, and microwave ovens mislead us into believing that things can be accomplished instantly.

Television sitcoms show troublesome relationships, financial difficulties, and life-threatening illnesses resolved within the thirty minutes, including commercial breaks, allotted for the program. These magical, simplistic solutions gloss over the reality that many of life's problems are complex and take years and years to be resolved. We can't rush these natural processes without destroying something vital and alive.

Sprouting

With the first green shoots, life mysteriously pushes up from the brown, crusted earth. This spurt of growth after a time of waiting is an encouraging sign that what I've done so far has worked.

The feelings that come with these first signs of growth are similar to those we feel when any new or unknown life venture shows signs of progressing. We feel energized and optimistic about the future.

Still, the thrill and excitement of having succeeded in planting seeds that germinate and sprout may leave us with a false sense of security. We cannot assume that from this point on our work has ended. Although the major physical effort we've put forth in the garden's creation is past, there is still much to be done.

Savoring each phase of the garden process is a reward in itself, but now it's time for us to move on. Later, as the garden continues through its cycle, there will be other natural stopping-off points when we can pause and reflect on what we've done.

Watering

To tell whether it's time to water, I test the top four inches of soil. I scoop up a handful of loam and find it dry. In the early morning when it's still cool and I can minimize water evaporation, I turn on the sprinkler for half an hour, thoroughly soaking the ground down to the roots of my plants. I've learned that the best rule of thumb is to water infrequently but deeply and thoroughly.

Some gardeners make the mistake of watering shallowly and often, believing that this type of attention will benefit their plants. But frequent, brief watering keeps root development near the surface of the soil.

Deep watering encourages root growth and enables plants to build reserves. With fully developed roots, they will be healthier and better able to survive periods of drought.

Loving relationships, too, require devotion, attention, and the time to develop at a deep level. And like deeply rooted plants that will survive deprivation and stress during times when water is scarce, friends, lovers, and family members can survive periods of difficulty by drawing sustenance from a storehouse of shared experience and deeply rooted inner emotional reserves.

In extreme situations where illness, infidelity, or financial losses attack the flowering or continuing life of a relationship above ground—when there may seem, on the surface of things, no reason to continue—it is the history of love and happiness, the deep roots of caring and shared experience, that can weather the time of crisis or drought.

Fertilizing

In addition to adequate water, air, and light, my garden plants need nutrients to carry them through their life cycle. Nitrogen, phosphorus, and potassium are the three main nutrients that they require in large amounts for consistent, healthy growth. Lack of these supplements will result in deformed or undersized plants.

The soil cannot supply all of the nutrients my plants need. I must add food in the form of compost or fertilizers. Compost, which consists of decomposed organic matter such as grass clippings, leaves, and vegetable kitchen refuse, breaks down slowly and is a complete food for the garden soil; it improves the soil's structure and replaces some depleted nutrients.

Fertilizers, which act more rapidly on plants than compost does, are packaged commercially in liquid or dried form. Nursery shelves are stocked with a bewildering variety of commercial fertilizers. Since my garden is an organic one, I eliminate from consideration those that are artificial and manufactured by chemical companies. I select only balanced, complete, organic fertilizers made of animal or plant remains such as fish or seaweed.

Part of the gardener's skill lies in understanding that plants have varying nutritional needs and in providing each

with a balanced feeding that meets its particular require-
ment. My rhododendrons are a good example of this need
to tailor the right blend of nutrients to the plant. I noticed
that they were doing poorly, that they had failed to flower
and the leaves had turned yellow. I researched the problem
and discovered that rhododendrons, which are native to the
Himalayas, need the acidic soil of the rainy forest floors
from which they originate. I'd been feeding them the liquid
fish fertilizer I gave the rest of the garden. I redug their
planting holes adding generous amounts of leaf mold and
peat moss. In a while the leaves turned green and the plants
flowered the following spring.

Growing for Emotional and Spiritual Balance

It is time, once again, to return to your garden sanctuary, to
that special place where you have found peace and relax-
ation. By now you probably know how to arrive there with
ease, either by saying the name you have given your Mind
Garden or by slowing your breathing and relaxing your
body.

Take in the sights, sounds, smells, and textures—all of
the variety in this garden you have created. Experience the
smell of the damp, rich soil warmed by the sun and the
faint perfume of the flowers. Notice all of the things that
are growing in your garden: the mature trees and shrubs in
full leaf, the young seedlings and the flowers in bud and
bloom. Think, too, of the growth soon to begin beneath
the furrows of freshly planted seed beds.

As you look around you, become aware of how each
thing in the garden is progressing at its own rate, in accor-
dance with Nature's plan. Each seed, each plant in your garden is unique and has its own germinating time. Although
you may have planted larkspur and zinnia seeds the same

day, the zinnias will germinate in a week, and the larkspur will take twice that amount of time to begin to grow.

From what we can observe about growth in the garden, we can see that we mustn't worry if some of our relationships, plans, and ideas take longer than others to evolve. Each thing conforms to its own organic pattern. We must appreciate this uniqueness and not fall into the trap of viewing growth as something mechanical and regimented that we can completely control.

As you continue to take stock of your garden, see if it is receiving enough water and fertilizer. Are the plants green and healthy, the flowers full and lush?

Thoroughly water the dry areas of your garden, making sure the plants drink deeply so that the roots and soil around them are drenched. Apply fertilizer or work compost into the soil around plants that are undersized or whose leaves are discolored.

When you've watered and fed your garden, paying attention to the individual needs of various plants, return the sprinkler, hose, and fertilizer to their storage space and take time to rest and reflect on the work that you have completed. In a short time, perhaps while you relax in your garden, wilted stems and leaves will spring back into shape. During the days and weeks to follow, you will feel more and more satisfaction as you watch the plants grow greener, sprouting new shoots and buds, the results of the watering and feeding you've done.

FIRST GARDEN

IN 1941, WHEN I was eight, my parents, brother, and I went to live with my grandmother in a crowded red-brick, two-family house in the West Bronx.

Below us, on the first floor, lived my great aunt. In addition, a small attic apartment was let to an overly friendly middle-aged widow who smelled of alcohol.

It was the tail end of the Depression and money was scarce. During the day, my grandmother kept house and looked after my brother and me while my mother worked as a bookkeeper. My ten-year-old brother, a wiry, cocky rooster of a boy, nicknamed the "King," resented being told what to do by my stocky, strong-willed grandmother.

I remember her, eyes flashing with anger, jaws set tight, twirling a dish towel into a weapon as she strode toward him across the kitchen floor. "You're not my mother," he would challenge with a smirk, his hands on his hips. Then, as my grandmother's face reddened with angry resolve and her pace quickened, my brother would dart through the door and escape down the stairs to the street.

Deeply affected by the currents of tension in the house and by the lack of privacy (I had to share a room with my brother), I sought refuge wherever I could find it.

Aside from the basement, where I found solitude when no one was using the washing machine or stoking the coal furnace, a small backyard was the only place I could go to be alone.

The garden was a sad little place. Sandwiched between two tall apartment buildings that cast long shadows, it received only a few hours of sun each day. Several scraggly rosebushes, a lilac, and some dusty hedges persisted in their struggle for life and occasionally put out a small bloom or two. Although most of the lawn had died, a few patches of tufted green clung tenaciously to the bare ground.

The rear window of Scheff's Bakery opened onto the backyard. In winter, air from the oven billowed in white, steamy clouds through a black, iron-grated window. I recall the smell of rye bread and bagels baking and, in summer, the feel of suffocating waves of hot, yeasty air.

The shaded garden, silent except for the background hum of street traffic and the racketing of an elevated train that ran above Jerome Avenue, became the sanctuary I sought.

On days I didn't feel like playing jacks or jumping rope on the sidewalk with my friends, I could be quiet, daydream, make up stories, and wait for my mother to come home.

One spring, when they sold seeds for five cents a packet in school, I bought some cosmos and snapdragons and tried growing them. I had a vision of a large bouquet I would pick to make my mother happy.

Using an old soupspoon for a shovel, I scooped out a straight row in the dry, hard soil, then planted and watered the seeds. But the moisture drained from the soil, and the seeds dried out. When they failed to germinate in the number of days printed on the seed packets, I gave up on them.

Then I discovered that someone had planted lily of the valley pips in deep shade near the back fence where they flourished unattended. In April, after the last of the frost had gone, I watched as each day their small, tender green tips pushed up from the leaf-strewn undergrowth of some philadelphus bushes.

The green shoots extended themselves, formed buds, and opened into perfect, white, nodding, perfumed bells.

When the handful of flowers were in full bloom, I gathered them into a nosegay that I tied with a ribbon and gave to my mother when she arrived home.

She smiled, patted me on the head, and then wearily turned her attention to the impossible task of making peace between my brother and grandmother. I arranged the flowers in a small vase and put them on a windowsill near the kitchen table.

Early the next morning when we were alone at breakfast, she picked up the vase and raised it to her nose. She closed her eyes, inhaling the delicious perfume. "These flowers remind me of May Day," she said.

Smiling wistfully, with a faraway look in her eyes, she told how, when she was a girl in Mount Vernon, on the first of May all of her friends gathered lilies of the valley, violets, and forget-me-nots and wove them into garlands for their hair.

They'd decorate a pole in the schoolyard with floral wreaths and ribbon streamers. Dressed in white, their crowns of flowers in place, streamers in hand, they'd circle the flower-wreathed maypole singing songs to celebrate the coming of spring.

"You should have seen it, all the flowers and so much fun." When she spoke, the worry had gone, and for a moment I could see that girl in a white dress reflected in her sparkling eyes.

In my meager little garden in the Bronx, I not only found peace and quiet, I also discovered the power of Nature. There I learned about survival and regeneration and how, in the effort to endure, some things are lost but others, against all odds, doggedly persist.

Sometimes I wonder about that garden and whether it still exists. But it really doesn't matter. Like my mother's May Day memory, it will always be there, somewhere in a corner of my mind.

6

TENDING

People seldom see the halting and painful steps by which the most insignificant success is achieved.

ANNIE SULLIVAN

T HE FIRST FLUSH OF EN-
thusiasm we've felt in designing and planting a new garden
may give way to boredom as we settle into the routines of
tending established plants. It's easy to tire of caregiving after
the dedicated watchfulness required in helping young seeds
and plants get started. We may mistakenly hope that things
in the garden can, with some water and fertilizer, mature on
their own.

Yet, while concentrated attention may no longer be
necessary, there is still much to do. To guide and shape the
garden, we must weed, prune, transplant, and control pests.
This kind of tending requires constancy and dedication.
While less dramatic than the initial birth of the garden and
less spectacular than its final flowering, the development
that occurs as we weed or prune is just as important to the
process as a whole.

Although weeding, cutting back, and transplanting are
activities that may seem repetitive and never-ending, when
seen as a necessary and integral part of the overall unfolding
of the garden scheme, they become purposeful rather than
boring.

In fact, what may appear on the surface to be tedious
physical work may, in the actual doing, be spiritually liber-
ating. In taking time to contemplate the small—in observing the details of our gardens—we can experience life on a
manageable scale.

As we pay close attention to what is happening around us, our powers of observation become keener and our awareness is heightened. As we weed, prune, transplant, and keep plants free of disease, we experience a sense of completion and satisfaction often lost in the complexity and fragmentation of daily life.

Weeding

Weeds are plants that have adapted themselves to survive under the harshest of conditions. Because of their resilience and tenacity, they can overwhelm our gardens unless we keep after them.

When possible, I weed a few days after a good downpour. Then the soil is not so dry that roots won't come free easily or too wet and muddy for me to be in the garden. I pull larger weeds by hand, but when roots are particularly deep, I use my spading fork. To remove smaller weeds, I use my hands or a small garden trowel.

In weeding we remove the extraneous. If we didn't weed our gardens, they would, in a short time, lose their definition and beauty. Perhaps this is why gardeners find weeding, although tedious to contemplate, so satisfying in the actual doing. With the uprooting of each weed, we are saying no to confusion and disorder and yes to clarity.

Some people find release in the act of weeding—an outlet for frustration or other negative emotions. A client of mine, caught up in a bureaucracy of social workers and courts as she struggled to regain custody of her children, told of how she would take her frustrated rage into the garden and "pull weeds right and left." After a while she would feel her anger subside as ordered beds and borders of flowers emerged from the tangle of weeds.

As we remove the unessential, we also rediscover each plant we've put in the ground. This is why I find that weeding by hand is best. It forces me to my knees, close to the earth and to each detail of the garden environment. When I look closely, I can quickly distinguish between weeds and plants, and in handling the leaves and flowers I notice new weed growth or snail damage before it has gone too far. I can stand back when finished and experience the immediate aesthetic rewards of having restored the harmony of shape, color, and design.

So often our weeding efforts are sporadic or haphazard, and we let things go until they are no longer manageable. If you are someone who doesn't complete projects or who procrastinates, try setting aside ten minutes each day to do the routine tasks you've been putting off. In a short time, you'll find that this small daily effort will begin to make a difference. Things will become more manageable. The routines themselves, rather than being tedious and oppressive, will become meditative and restful and will provide you with a chance to slow down and connect with yourself.

If you make a daily habit of this kind of tending, not only will the chores at hand become more manageable but you may experience a general sense of grounding and relief from tension.

Pruning

When we prune, we remove the stems, branches, or roots of a tree or shrub. We do so to modify a plant's shape, to remove dead or injured parts, or to foster growth and improve the quality of the plant's fruits and flowers.

I prune my rosebushes in late winter or early spring, while they are dormant. Without leaves and flowers, the basic shape of the plant is easier to see, and I can make my cuts artfully and symmetrically.

Using pruning shears, I first remove the dead canes, cutting them to the base of the plant. Then I shape the rest of the bushes by removing canes and branches that are spindly and that interfere with the plant's optimal shape.

If I want more flowers, I prune the tops of canes by making a clean cut at a forty-five-degree angle from a bud, slanting in an upward direction. This is a job to be done with care, both in deciding which cuts to make and in avoiding the bush's sharp thorns.

For some, who let growth go unchecked until limbs and branches cover walkways or reach into neighbors' yards, pruning becomes a dreaded chore. Eager to complete the task, they hastily hack away, leaving a jumble of ragged stems, scarred limbs, and stumps. Future flowering and fruiting are inhibited, and the very survival of the plants may be jeopardized. Pruning should be an act of encouraging healthy, pleasing growth, rather than simply a way to get rid of an annoyance.

In contrast to weeding, which gives immediate aesthetic satisfaction, pruning demands from us a leap of faith. Even when we prune properly, branches and stems may look barren when we've finished cutting them back. We may find ourselves reluctant to begin because we don't want to face the possibility of denuding the garden.

Yet this temporary loss will result in long-term gain. Although, after pruning, trees and shrubs may look bare and truncated, in the long run they'll be more shapely and healthy. During the blooming season as well, in removing dead flower heads, we prevent the plant from spending its energies ripening seed, and we encourage it to produce more of the colorful flowers we've enjoyed throughout the season. Removing the brown, spent blooms from my marguerites not only keeps the existing mounds of daisies tidy but also ensures a steady supply of new buds.

Because I like large roses, I pinch off the smaller of the three or four buds that form on each stem of my hybrid tea-rose bush and leave only the largest one. This enables the plant to devote its energies to producing one huge, splendid, creamy yellow rose to a stem.

In our own lives, we must cut back on activities and interests when we've branched out in too many directions or scattered too much of our energy. Deciding what and where to prune back may be difficult if you are someone who has many interests and responsibilities. In being selective and encouraging the things that are most important to you, you will avoid the undisciplined expenditure of your life energies, and you will actually accomplish more in the long run.

As I reflect on this need to cut back and make choices, I am reminded of Ansel Adams, who, realizing he could not become a truly great artist in two areas, abandoned his career as a concert pianist to devote himself completely to photography. This is what he says in his autobiography about making the choice:

> During the first two years of our marriage I juggled two professions: music and photography. By 1930 I was wracked by indecision because I could not afford either emotionally or financially to continue splitting my time between them. I decided to return to New Mexico to complete the Taos book, hoping the Southwest summer sunlight and towering thunderclouds would inspire a decision.

While in New Mexico, Adams met the photographer Paul Strand, who showed him some of his negatives:

My understanding of photography was crystallized that afternoon as I realized the great potential of the medium as an expressive art. I returned to San Francisco resolved that the camera, not the piano, would shape my destiny.

Transplanting

The evolution of the garden necessitates change, movement, and rearrangement. Gardeners make mistakes that they need to remedy, plants outgrow their spaces, tastes and conditions change.

Recently I had to move a fig tree that I'd planted two years before in a small corner of my yard. When it grew by leaps and bounds, I realized that in locating such a vigorous tree in such a small space, I'd allowed my love of figs to get the better of my judgment. I had planned to keep the tree in check by pruning, but when it grew even larger than expected, I saw that it would have to be moved. The matter took on some urgency when, during the course of enlarging a room in my house, I needed more yard space.

Fortunately, I was able to find a friend who wanted the tree and had room to plant it in her yard. We set a date to move it the following week.

Although it would have been best to move the fig when it was dormant, I was going to have to transplant now, in May, after it had leafed out. The move would require some planning to ensure the tree's survival. To make digging easy and keep the root ball firm, three days before the move I scooped a wide saucer-shaped depression around the tree and thoroughly soaked the soil with water.

Using the breadth of the treetop as a guide for estimating the size of the root ball, my friend dug a large planting hole in the sunny open space she'd chosen for the tree. She then mixed compost in with the soil she'd excavated.

On the day of the move, we dug up the soil around the fig tree, being careful not to break the roots. Then we gently lifted the tree, its root ball intact, onto a piece of burlap, which we folded around the root ball and tied with string. We carried the balled tree to a waiting car and delivered it to its new location.

Here we slid the burlap from under the dampened root ball and set the tree in the planting hole. This we filled with fresh loam, which we gently tamped, creating a saucer-shaped depression around the base of the tree. We completed the job by soaking the roots with a mixture of water and vitamin B_1.

As a result of the forethought, planning, and care we gave to relocating the fig tree, it took to its new environment without suffering any damage. In fact, that same season, to the delight of my friend, it bore several figs.

Whenever we disturb roots, whether in the course of planting tender young seedlings or transplanting established shrubs or trees, we have to take special care. Roots are the heart of the plant. Stems, leaves, and branches can grow again but, once the roots die, the plant dies, too.

When we ourselves become "root bound" and have outgrown our potential in a given situation, we need to change, to move on. To ensure our continued growth, we may find it necessary to leave places, jobs, and relationships and spread our roots in more fertile soil.

As we contemplate a new direction, we must be aware of the import of uprooting established things—family, friends, routines—and how vulnerable these changes may make us. This is an important time to strengthen the bonds of friendship and love with those we cherish and rely on. Telephone calls, letters, and visits can help us through times of transition.

Studies have shown that events such as divorce, job change, and moving significantly increase stress and our chances of becoming ill. Knowing our vulnerability at these times and preparing for transitions in advance can reduce the likelihood of trauma and disorientation.

Pest Management

Insects are vital to the garden. They pollinate plants, aerate soil, provide food for birds, and help to control other insects that are harmful to plants.

The temporary intervention of the gardener to remove insects is necessary only when pests begin to do severe damage. But because most of us spend so much time in cities where we come in contact with few insects other than ants and cockroaches, we generally view all insects as adversaries—carriers of disease that invade territories that belong to us. We know little of the benefits that many insects bring to the garden and of their natural place in its ecosystem.

In my garden I intervene only when pests begin to do severe damage. Each year after the heavy winter rains, snails nest and breed in my iris clumps. They multiply rapidly and, if left unchecked, strip the leaves as they feed, sapping the plants of energy. I've found the easiest way to control them is to pick them off by hand.

In other instances, I use water to control garden pests. When aphids cover my rosebushes in spring in such vast numbers that they threaten the survival of the buds, I use a jet spray from my hose to flush them off.

Making sure plants are well watered and fed and that debris around them, where insects may breed, is cleared helps to strengthen plants and makes them less susceptible to damage from insects. When pests persist in attacking a plant, I may replace it with a variety better adapted to my growing area and the conditions of my garden.

When a problem persists, don't give in to the temptation to eradicate pests with a blast of poisonous insecticide. This kind of intervention will give immediate relief but will make for other problems down the road.

Pesticides kill harmful insects, but they also destroy others necessary to the ecosystem of our gardens. Praying mantises, which feed on garden pests, and bees, which pollinate flowers, die when pesticides are used. Also, poisons are absorbed not only by the plants and soil but by our skin and lungs.

I've learned that I can't control everything in my garden, and I always leave some room for insects. Unless damage to plants is unreasonable, a tattered leaf here and there is a sign that my garden includes other living things besides plants, as it should.

When I allow space for other creatures to coexist, controlling pests becomes not a chore but an opportunity to learn. In your garden, learn to observe the bugs. Wonder about them. Contemplate their place in Nature. Try not to think of them as things to be killed.

A sterile, bugless garden is an unhealthy garden. Humans, plants, insects—we are interdependent, part of a universal system.

Overtending

If you have a tendency to work too hard, try to avoid this pattern as you garden, for you will end up perpetually weeding, trimming, and pruning. While it's important to tend your garden, it is also important to relax there, to observe the plants as they grow, and to experience the communion with Nature that is the special delight gardening offers.

In allowing some climbing roses to roam free or some forget-me-nots to run a bit rampant, in letting some colorful autumn leaves settle on the lawn, you allow the plants to express themselves, and you avoid the monotonous predictability that results from a perfectly trimmed and edged garden.

We mustn't be too quick to remove a plant that has passed the peak of its bloom. Some are quite attractive even in their waning—much prettier and more interesting than the bare brown bed of soil that would be left if they were removed. And we mustn't forget the added benefit that comes as plants complete their cycle of growth and form seeds that draw birds to our gardens.

The way you tend your garden can tell you a lot about how you deal with your own human nature. Are you overzealous? Do you feel you always need to take charge of things? Is it hard for you to let things flower in their own way?

Try loosening your need for control and allowing things to take their course. If you've been keeping your hedges perfectly manicured, try letting them grow for a while. An untrimmed privet hedge will produce fragrant white flowers that will delight and surprise you. Bees love the nectar of the flowers and will come to feed. Bee watching in the flower-scented air will enliven your senses and help you to slow down and find relief from burdensome responsibilities.

Tending for Emotional and Spiritual Balance

It's time, once again, to visit your Mind Garden. Find a quiet place where you can close your eyes and relax. Slow your breathing, release any tension you are feeling in your body, and bring yourself to the garden sanctuary you have created.

When you've arrived, stroll through your garden, observing the growth that has taken place since your last visit. By now the seedlings and seeds you planted, fed, and watered have taken hold. Stems have thickened and grown, leaves and branches have multiplied. Trees, bushes, and shrubs have sunk deep roots and spread in many directions. As growth progresses in your garden, you will need to protect and encourage your plants.

As you glance around, observe places where weeds have begun to grow and decide whether you want to remove them now. If you haven't visited your Mind Garden for a while, you may find that there will be quite a bit of weeding to do. Don't worry—if you take your time and work in a relaxed manner, you'll find that your efforts will be rewarded. As you dig up weeds, you'll feel the satisfaction of restoring order and definition to your garden. As you root out problems in the garden, you will bring calm and order to your mind.

As you look further at your garden, you may notice that trees and shrubs have developed overlapping branches or become lopsided or top-heavy. If you like, spend time pruning the undesired growth, shaping the trees and shrubs to the contours that are pleasing to you and healthful for the plant. Continue through your garden noting other tending needs.

Although the various activities of tending may require a good deal of your attention, be careful not to overwork yourself. You may do your tending in increments. Be aware of the limits of your energy and proceed slowly but steadily. Stop whenever your inner voice tells you to, and resume your tending tasks when you have more time and feel more able, always remembering that mind gardening is an activity to be done at your own natural place.

If you haven't time to complete all you'd like to during this visit, take stock of what remains to be done and make plans to return when you have more time. Remember that this is your garden. You have created it, and it exists just for you.

If you find that taking care of your garden is too much work, you may want to stop to rethink your plan. Perhaps you have made the garden too large. If this is the case, try scaling it down. A simple garden can still give much pleasure.

If you find yourself repeating compulsive patterns, having to manicure your garden, or competing for the biggest and the best in your neighborhood and pushing yourself to the point of exhaustion, stop to reflect on your actions.

It may be time for you to reevaluate the way you do things.

Here in your Mind Garden you can learn to do things differently. Allow your breath to tell you when things are right for you, your body to tell you when to rest and when to proceed. The way you tend your garden and the way you tend to your own needs are one and the same.

THE FENCE

 THE OPENING LINE of Robert Frost's poem "Mending Wall" reads, "Something there is that doesn't love a wall."

To write such words, he couldn't possibly have grown up in New York City (as I did) or had an older brother (like mine) who took away his toys and disrupted the games he played. I have always appreciated walls, doors, and fences.

When I moved into the house on Jasper Avenue eight years ago, the spacious yard was overgrown with weeds and strewn with rubble. A fence made of faded, whitewashed cedar ran along three sides of the property, separating my house from neighbors to the east, south, and west. The portion that marked the southern and eastern boundaries had been gnawed by termites until the wood had broken off at the soil line. Depending on where one looked along its expanse, the fence was in a state of either gradual or total collapse. I wanted to find a way to replace it, but I didn't have the money.

Directly to the south, through spaces left by fallen fence slats, I could see a grassless backyard paved completely in concrete. It was populated by several garishly colored plastic ducks and a pair of life-sized, brown plaster deer that stood frozen in the Southern California sun. Pots of artificial roses and ferns were spaced at regular intervals on the pavement, and red artificial geraniums cascaded awkwardly from the top of a stone wall erected for privacy around a hot tub. Early each morning a middle-aged couple, who spoke to one another in a foreign language, swept the concrete and hosed down the plants and animals.

Along the western boundary, the fence zigzagged, first leaning into my yard and then under some peach trees on the property next door.

All of these openings in the fence made me uneasy. I didn't like the idea that anyone could walk, uninvited, into my yard.

Some of my discomfort was allayed when, shortly after I moved in, the neighbors with the plastic flowers replaced the fallen fence along their property with a six-foot-tall cinder block wall.

After that, the only remaining gap was along the western edge of the property, where the peach trees grew. Through the broken fence slats, I could see a lush, green backyard with mature trees and shrubs. Unlike my recently landscaped garden, which had many carefully arranged young plants, the one next door was more casually tended and a bit overgrown.

One morning, as I was working in the yard, a small, soft-spoken woman with long brown hair and faded jeans appeared at the fence. She said her name, "Sharon," as she handed me two avocados she'd picked from a large tree that stood behind her. We talked for a while, and I learned that she was a single parent with three children.

We discovered that we were both avid gardeners. We laughed about the concrete yard with its plastic plants and shared our relief over the newly built wall.

Our conversation shifted to the fence between our properties. We talked about its decrepitude and bemoaned the fact that neither of us could afford to replace it, even if we shared the expense.

After that, when we gardened, we'd often meet at the rickety fence near the peach trees and chat. We exchanged plants and news of our gardens. This sharing seemed to bring Sharon some particular pleasure, and one day she suggested that we tear down the leaning fence and open our gardens to one another.

I told her I'd have to think about it. As much as I liked her, I wondered if I'd lose my sense of privacy and the individuality of my garden if we removed the fence.

The following winter we had unusually heavy winds and rains, and the old fence finally fell to the ground. When the weather cleared, Sharon and I bundled up the debris and put it out with the trash during the sanitation department's "Spring Cleanup Week."

The landscaping on either side of the fence had been ruined when it fell. But once we'd cleared the trampled plants, an unexpected change took place. Where before I'd been able to see only the tops of the blossom-covered peach trees, I now had a full view of them, and they provided a handsome, much-needed background for the flowers in my treeless garden.

Elated over the potential of a shared garden space, Sharon volunteered some paving stones. Sparked by her enthusiasm, I contributed some bricks, and we worked together to make a path connecting our gardens and to redo the landscaping crushed by the fallen fence.

My feared loss of privacy was never realized. Where I had feared invasion, I received help and consideration for my needs instead. Just after dawn one morning, when the garden snails were out in full force, I came across Sharon and her son Mark in my backyard collecting them in glass jars. "I hope it's all right. We looked into your yard after we'd finished in our garden and thought we might as well continue over here." They knew how much I hated killing snails.

Many other kindnesses followed throughout the seven years that we were neighbors. We regularly walked the path between our yards to borrow garden tools, to exchange flowers or vegetables, or just to visit. Yet each of our gardens was still our own and expressed our individual styles.

Both of us have since moved on to other places and to other gardens, but neither of us has forgotten the special relationship that grew as a result of a fallen fence we couldn't afford to replace.

Sharon is in the process of landscaping the garden of an old house she's restoring. I got a letter from her recently saying how much she misses me and how unfriendly her new neighbor is. Then she thanked me for all she had learned from me about gardening.

When I write to her, I want to be sure to send thanks, too. But mine will be for her determination to join gardens with me in spite of my reluctance; in so doing, she helped me to break down an old wall of distrust.

Maybe Robert Frost was right, after all.

7

CONSERVING

Over increasingly large areas of the United States,
spring now comes unheralded by the return of the birds,
and early mornings are strangely silent where once
they were filled with the beauty of bird song.

RACHEL CARSON

SUNDAY MORNING. CUP OF coffee in hand, I sit at the kitchen table gazing out my window into the backyard.

The coming of a new day has set the garden in motion. Sun-warmed air turns droplets of dew into vapory mist. Small insects catch the light as they flit through the air. Crinkled poppies unfolding from the night lift orange cups to the sun.

A monarch butterfly rests on a leaf, flicking its wings, while bees nearby gather nectar from roses. On the ground, small sparrows peck at seeds. The scent of lilacs fills the room. In the golden quiet of the morning, I am content.

A few moments later I open the Sunday paper and begin to read. My serenity fades as the headline announces another oil spill. This one has washed onto the beach of a resort town in Southern California. An accompanying photograph shows dead birds on the oil-blackened sand—a familiar sight now, as oil spills large and small are a constant in the news. A sinking feeling comes over me as yet another environmental tragedy becomes routine, as the unthinkable becomes commonplace.

On the bottom of the back page, I come across an article that reports that as the destruction of the rain forests of South America proceeds, one plant species becomes extinct each day. With the passing of each of these species, which took millions of years to evolve, goes part of the diversity and variety of life around us. These losses threaten the complex web of life that holds the key to our survival. It seems this should be a front-page headline, not a small news item tucked into a corner of the back page!

I feel depressed and overwhelmed, then powerless and helpless as I contemplate the enormity of these problems. What can I, one person, do about the contamination and destruction of life on earth?

Outside my window lies my garden, so alive, so green, and thriving. How can this be? Is it an illusion? This little microcosm—how does it relate to the larger world? Can it or I make a difference?

As I reflect on what I've learned through gardening, I answer my own question. The way *is* through the garden. I came to the garden ill, exhausted, not knowing how to conserve my own energies, let alone those of the earth. I recall how, in the quiet, I found a way to reconnect with my own nature and with Nature around me. I learned to conserve and balance my own energies—to heal and renew myself.

My garden has become an informal classroom, a kind of laboratory where I learn vital things overlooked in my formal education. In school, I had the feeling that my head was being filled with information, while my heart, feelings, and intuition—my basic human nature—were devalued and neglected. I felt that I was being trained simply to memorize things by rote, to perform tasks.

I experienced the same disjointedness and fragmentation when I later went to work and my days were spent in a stuffy windowless cubicle far from Nature. Just surviving seemed to take up all of my time and energy. The feeling that something wasn't right persisted, even as I advanced professionally and became "successful."

Then I found my way to the garden. In the calm and quiet, at one with the plants and the soil, I began to experience a connectedness and inner balance I had not found elsewhere.

The truths I found were amazingly simple. Each gardening activity grew naturally out of the last. As I interacted with plants, soil, sky, birds, and insects, I felt my very being pulsing in time to Nature's rhythms.

As I regained my health, I came to understand that I was not the only victim of this alienation from Nature. I saw that others—in fact, our entire society—were suffering as well.

But the solution is simpler, gentler than the problem. It is easy to conserve, to balance your intake with your output, to recycle and restore to the earth what you take from it.

Once again, I invite you into my garden.

Composting

When I'm composting, I'm returning to a tradition of the past when our foremothers routinely collected kitchen scraps and added them to the compost heap. In order to conserve, I've had to change some habits. Instead of tossing organic kitchen waste into the trash, I now put it in a covered container I keep near the sink.

Today I gather up orange peels and eggshells from breakfast and add them to the scraps I've saved over the past couple of days. I step outside and make my twice-weekly pilgrimage to the compost heap.

Compost is vegetable kitchen refuse, leaves, clippings, and other garden debris onto which we add layers of garden soil, manure, and enough water to keep it damp. The pile is turned about once a week as it decomposes.

Some compost heaps are housed in elaborately constructed bins, but mine is a simple circle of wire held in place by wooden stakes. I've located it out of view between the back fence and a large juniper.

This morning, I toss my kitchen scraps on the heap and then, using a pitchfork to turn the layers, add some soil and water. The compost heap gives off a pungent odor. It took me a while to get used to the smell, accustomed as I am to a world in which natural odors are often masked with perfume. But now I've come to like the earthy smell of the compost heap. To me, it is a sign that living matter is breaking down and regenerating.

When the compost has turned brown and broken into small pieces, it's ready for use. I periodically add it to my garden soil to improve its texture.

In the compost heap we can see the life cycle. As the leaves, potato peels, orange skins, and grass clippings decompose, we can observe the relationship of decay to regeneration.

While I turn the layers, I reflect on how a similar process takes place in our minds. Just as we turn the organic matter in the compost heap, recycling it over time, we sift and turn the layers of our own raw experience. The passage of time and our reflective thought transform this experience into knowledge and wisdom.

A painful event such as a divorce or the loss of a job may, when it first happens, seem traumatic or grim. Over time as we come to terms with our grief, we can actually see our initial feelings transformed into something new.

Composting also demonstrates to me the value of economy and how, in a small way, I can control my environment and eliminate wasteful practices. Since I make my own compost, I don't need to have my garden waste hauled away, nor do I have to buy expensive soil amendments. Then, there is beauty and an elegant simplicity in utilizing the bits and scraps of things that I consume. In Nature, nothing is wasted.

When we recycle human-made materials, we continue this process of conservation.

Recycling

We've at last come back to the age-old tradition of recycling. Recycling, like composting, was something our grandparents did as a matter of course. Now we are recognizing that these priorities of the past have value.

Using surplus or salvaged construction material is a great way to conserve. Paths, gates, and fences made with used railroad ties, brick, stone, and wood add character to your garden.

Recycling "found" objects and materials into your garden stimulates invention in ways that new, more expensive, mass-manufactured items don't. For a circular path in a large flower garden, I collected used brick from demolition sites. The odd sizes and various colors of brick made a charming patchwork walk. Although the garden was new, the recycled brick gave it a look of permanence, and I was pleased to have some reminders of the old neighborhood that was now rapidly changing.

Used tires make ideal raised planters. You can plant seedlings in the center opening. As the plants mature, they will conceal the rubber with their leaves and flowers. Similarly, small plastic food containers can be used to start seeds that will later be transplanted to the garden.

Another way we can recycle is to use "gray" water, water that has previously been used for bathing and laundry. It can be siphoned from bathtubs and washing machines into the garden. And there are other ways to conserve water as well.

Water Conservation

In or out of the garden, water is our most precious resource. Life on earth depends on it.

I think of conserving water in three ways: by avoiding leakage, preventing runoff, and minimizing evaporation.

With awareness and some strategic planning, we can prevent each of these potential losses.

You should check regularly for leaks in pipes and hoses, patching or replacing as needed. Dripping faucets and hose nozzles are a sign that it's time to put in new washers. Sprinkler heads and the hoses and pipes in the sprinkler system should also be checked. If they become clogged with mineral or soil particles, water flow will be blocked and the hose or pipe may burst.

One way to prevent runoff is to collect rainwater that would otherwise drain into sewers or evaporate from puddles on the ground. Everyone used to have a wooden rain barrel for this purpose. You can revive this old custom by making your own rain barrel out of a large garbage can. Place it under a shortened downspout of a roof gutter and use the water for the garden.

Terracing sloped or hilly land is another way to prevent water loss. When we terrace, we cut graded steps into a hillside. By creating leveled steps out of the slope and by reinforcing the dirt edges with stone or wood, we slow the rate of runoff and maximize water absorption.

If you don't want to terrace, you can reinforce a slope with sandbags or large rocks, or you can use ground covers to hold the soil in place. Choices among ground covers vary from evergreens such as Boston ivy to colorful tropicals such as bougainvillea and lantana, which make handsome displays as they cascade down hillsides. Seeding annual grasses and wildflowers on sloping land also helps to anchor the soil and prevent runoff.

It's easy for moisture in soil and plants to evaporate. As a general rule, I water my plants only in the early morning or in the evening, or when it's cloudy and the sun's rays are weak; this keeps evaporation to a minimum.

Mulching, the practice of putting a mixture of compost, wood chips, grass clippings, or sawdust on the soil at the base of plants, is something I do routinely. It not only keeps water in the soil but holds down weed growth as well, saving me time and work.

In addition, I can keep the garden moist by planting ground cover in place of pavement. In this way the earth absorbs rainwater, which would otherwise evaporate or run off, and replenishes the underground freshwater supply.

Selecting plants that are native to your area or ones that require little water is another way of conserving water.

Changing the Way We Think

Conservation doesn't stop in the garden. What we learn to do in our gardens we must carry over into our family relationships, our communities, and the larger world.

The garden is a microcosm where we can glimpse a way of life in which humans and Nature are in balance—one in which we have a reciprocal relationship with the earth—where we are not just taking but are conserving and replenishing.

So, really, conservation is a frame of mind—one that we can adopt right now, right here. We don't have to fantasize about living in a different society. We don't all need to leave our jobs and move to the country. We can change things right where we are, begin to carve out green spaces where we live and work. We can insist that our home and work spaces meet our human needs and those of the plant and animal world of which we are a part.

It's not too late, and your efforts will not be too little.

All of the great social and political movements in history came about through the synchronicity of the will and the need of ordinary people.

Sometimes it's hard to make changes. The organizations listed in the appendix will give you some ways to connect with similarly oriented people.

Conserving for Emotional and Spiritual Balance

It's time now to take a moment to rest and renew yourself. Find a comfortable, quiet place where you can put aside the tensions and obligations of the day and pay a visit to your Mind Garden.

In preparation for your return, close your eyes and take some deep breaths as you relax your body and slow your pace. Then travel the path that leads you to that special garden space you have made for yourself.

Are there places in your life where your energies and efforts are being wasted? Perhaps one of your goals remains beyond your reach as your energies drain, your confidence shrivels, and your strength and determination erode.

Are you feeling depleted by a relationship in which you are giving a lot and getting little in return? Do you find yourself overwhelmed by tedious details at work and losing your enthusiasm and creativity? Are your own life energies leaking, wearing away, and drying up? Think of ways you can conserve life energies that are presently being wasted.

Take a moment to think of where you can cut back on useless expenditure of energy in your own life. Are you spending your days hurrying from dawn to dusk? Are you getting enough return for your efforts? You may want to stop and rethink the way you do things.

As you eliminate waste and learn to use your personal resources more effectively, you will reduce stress and be able to find time for reflection and for experiencing the spiritual aspects of life. You will be able to see yourself as a part of Nature, drawing sustenance from the earth and the community of family and friends around you. How important it is to our emotional, physical, and spiritual health to identify our true needs and to balance them wisely against the demands of survival.

LATE SUMMER GARDEN

THE COOL BREEZE that blows in from the sea these early September afternoons, shorter days, and the heavy dew of crisp, clear mornings signal the end of summer.

I glance out the front window at the tall palm across the street and make note of a new silence. The chattering birds that roosted in the large, dense fronds since spring have gone. In the west the sun is lower in the sky, its rays are slanted and thin, its narrowing arc proceeding slowly downward toward autumn.

I feel a drawing in within me, a sadness I cannot name. A nudge toward winter. My toes feel cold.

The sweet gum tree in my neighbor's yard, symmetrical and green in summer, the trim standard-bearer of an otherwise raggle-taggle garden, is now touched erratically by the red and russet brush of fall. There is no symmetry in autumn.

On the concrete pavement, green and yellow curls of leaves from a tree I do not know are swept into a twirling, rustling dance choreographed by the rise and fall of the wind.

It's time to start thinking of the winter garden. Yet something in me is not ready. Although the untidiness of the front yard nags at me, I haven't felt the heart surge necessary to tackle the snarl of fallen plants and faded flowers that sprawl across the old stone path leading to the side yard. The mixture of dead stems and still-blooming flowers presents a different beauty, a backward-and-forward one, life and death in one view, the past mixed in with the present.

The clarkia are now stiff, pale, umber stalks, their seed-pods dried and empty. The cosmos, well past the peak of their pink and magenta bloom, small flowers on the vis-caria. Garden afterthoughts, I think. Lavender starlets peek out beneath the mother plant wasting above. I pity them their late and modest bloom. Not everything has a chance to reach fruition. I think of my own plans, my ideas that fail to mature, just like these last blooms.

I sit by the window looking out on the garden and recall the procession of bulb, seedling, and flowering shrub that has come and gone: the short and the tall, the pale and the vivid, stark leaved and frilled blossomed iris, cineraria, lark-spur, azalea, rhododendron, and sweet william. I need this time of resting and waning—an interlude in which to re-flect on the brilliance, to absorb and assimilate the light, the combinations of form and hue, the afterglow of unfolding seasons.

Before clearing, do we need to watch things go? Absorb the ending? Let the death sink in?

A soda bottle tossed by a passerby lies in the garden, and some newspaper blown in by the wind leans against a clump of irises. I let them remain.

Sometimes there is a need to hold onto the clutter, the debris of a relationship or a confusion. We can't be rushed. We need time to follow a cycle to its completion. We need time to sort out and make order, to absorb and integrate the meaning of an ending. When the time is right to move on, we feel it.

I think I'm waiting for the first heavy rain, which usu-ally comes in late October. Then the last of the flowers will fall and the stalks will rot. There will no longer be any rea-son for delay.

8

REFLECTING ON CATASTROPHE

AND LOSS

*In the depth of winter, I finally learned
that within me there lay an invincible summer.*

ALBERT CAMUS

I N THE GARDEN WE EXER-
cise control over Nature. We arrange its forms and exploit
its processes for beauty, sustenance, and sanctuary. When
elemental forces assert themselves and the fragile environ-
ments we have constructed are threatened or destroyed, we
quickly realize that this control is illusory.

Life in the garden, like life anywhere, is a set of unknowns to be explored, experienced, and understood.
Within the garden's natural growth cycles there arise random, unpredictable events that can bring catastrophe and
loss. Powerful winds may strip leaves, snap limbs, and down
trees. An unseasonable frost may kill tender plants and
freeze soil. Heavy rains may wash away topsoil and flood
plants. Prolonged drought may sear or burn vegetation.
Animals or vandals may trample or steal plantings.

Not all catastrophic loss is dramatic and sudden. It can
be gradual, subtle, and hidden. Plant diseases and pests
can infest and destroy from below. Roots can rot or be
eaten by gophers. Viruses may attack the cells of a plant
and waste it slowly from within.

When catastrophe strikes, initially we feel shock and dismay as favorite plants, some of which we've grown from
seeds and seedlings, are killed or injured. As we absorb the
full extent of the damage, we react with feelings of disbe-
lief, helplessness, anger, and sorrow.

You may feel overwhelmed and worried that you
won't be able to replace the trees and shrubs that have been

destroyed. Or you may feel frustrated that after having worked so hard, you'll have to begin again.

Reactions such as these are to be expected as you try to regain your equilibrium in the disorienting wake of catastrophe. With time, as you see how the garden naturally renews itself, you'll come to accept your losses, and you'll find within yourself the strength and enthusiasm to plant and grow again.

Responding to Loss

Different kinds of catastrophes call for different responses. A tree blown down by a storm may threaten a house, a power line, or the entire garden. A viral disease may spread rapidly from one plant to another. In such cases, we need to take immediate steps to cut down the fallen tree or remove the sickly plant.

At other times we may have difficulty determining the extent of the damage. When this is the case, it is best to let things sit for a while.

One winter, an unusually severe frost devastated a trumpet vine that grew along a thirty-foot length of my backyard fence. Over the weeks I watched the leaves shrivel and fade. I kept a watchful eye on the bare network of stems that clung to the fence to see if they would put out new growth, but they, too, withered and turned brown. I still couldn't tell if the roots had succumbed to the cold, so I cut down the dead stems and waited some more. My patience paid off, and in spring the vine put out new shoots. It grew so vigorously that by the end of summer it once again covered the fence.

In Nature, sometimes the things we least expect to survive regenerate in time. We were able to see this resilience demonstrated on a grand scale in the aftermath of the volcanic eruption of Mount Saint Helens in 1980.

Lava flows decimated all life on the surface of the mountain's slopes. Yet gophers living beneath the ground were insulated from the inferno. Over time their burrowing brought buried seeds to the surface where they subsequently germinated. The mounds of soil and volcanic ash that the gophers kicked up also trapped seeds blown in on the wind.

Now, about two decades after the eruption, the slopes are covered with dandelion, vine maple, and fireweed. Tree seedlings are growing out of decaying logs along streambeds.

The lava-covered hillsides are once again green.

Even when losses in our gardens are irreversible, we may decide to leave things as they are for a while and not replace the plants. Sometimes we need time to adapt, to let the garden soil rest, be rained on, and renewed.

During the night, strong winds of a March storm uprooted a favorite old plum tree. The tree was in full bud, just about to burst into clouds of white bloom.

I was heartsick when I saw it lying on the front lawn. Before I had the tree cut up for firewood, I saved a few of its branches and put them in water. They bloomed indoors. When I look at the bare spot where the gnarled tree once stood, I think about how much I loved it. I burned its wood in my fireplace last winter and thought about sweet, dark purple plums. I'm not yet ready to plant something else in its place.

Recovery

A haiku by the poet Issa expresses the paradoxical nature of life and death:

> A world of grief and pain:
> Flowers bloom,
> Even then.

With time, we clear away or dig under those plants we've lost. As the air and soil warm, scarred tree limbs put forth new branches, buds, and leaves. It is time for us to think of what to plant in the empty spaces.

Several years ago while serving on the program committee of a non-profit organization, I met a woman named Marion who had recently been widowed. She and her husband had been traveling in Europe six months earlier when he had died suddenly of a heart attack.

While she worked hard at keeping busy, her manner was subdued and detached, as though she were just going through the motions of filling her days. The wound of her loss was still fresh, and she needed to talk. Her conversation revolved around Jack and how close they'd been. She told me they'd met while they were in law school. Although both of them graduated and passed the bar, Marion had never practiced law. Following graduation she and Jack married. He became a practicing attorney, while Marion stayed home to raise their two children.

I lost touch with Marion when I moved to Northern California, but several years later we met again at a mutual friend's house while I was visiting Los Angeles.

She seemed totally changed, not so much in physical appearance as in her manner, which now exuded confidence, warmth, and enthusiasm.

As we reminisced about our shared past, Marion talked of how lost she'd felt in her grief and of how difficult that period of time had been. She'd counted on Jack to be there, and his death had left a void that was painful to confront. Then one day she saw a newspaper article describing how a cutback in funding was about to eliminate legal services for low-income women.

Marion went on to explain that for the past four years she had been practicing law. With a friend who was also widowed, she had established a nonprofit agency that provides legal services to low-income women.

"You know," Marion said, "Time really is a great healer. When Jack died I thought I wouldn't survive long without him. I still miss him very much. But I've made a rich and satisfying life for myself doing something I'd never in a million years have done had he lived—one door closes and another one opens."

Catastrophic events are a part of life: A thunderstorm brings needed rain. A forest fire that may appear to be a disaster is also a natural event that clears old growth and releases new seeds. Things come apart, break down, reform, and in time come together again, often with unexpected results.

Suffering and loss make us plumb the depths of our emotions. In going inward to reflect on and contemplate the meaning of our experience, we become wiser and better able to cope with life's adversities.

Restoring

If catastrophe or the disruption of order is part of the nature of things, then so, too, is restoration—the process of repairing and reordering what has been damaged or destroyed.

Over time, as damaged plants regenerate and we replace lost ones, integrating new colors and shapes into the garden, we see our overall plan reemerge. Through this reordering we regain a sense of unity and continuity.

Restoring can be more than just replacing what you've lost with the same or similar things. You can think about restoration in a broader sense, as a way in which you can have an impact on the larger environment. While you are down on your knees in the dirt, you can be doing something to help restore the planet.

By planting trees and shrubs, you help counteract the "greenhouse effect." Green leaves absorb the carbon dioxide produced by exhaust fumes and release the oxygen we need to breathe.

Your garden can be a place where you encourage, support, and protect rare plants and insects. If you enjoy exotic plants, you might have a collection of rare orchids, or you might fill your garden with endangered plants that are native to your area.

If you are interested in attracting butterflies, you can plant a "butterfly garden" by growing the plants they feed on. The same is true of particular birds native to your area. The bibliography at the end of this book lists publications that will help you create a special garden.

You might make a nostalgia garden in which you conserve and restore memories of the past. As we exchange plants with friends and neighbors over the years or acquire them through circumstances that are special to us, many of our gardens take on added significance.

One day as I was walking in my neighborhood, I passed a woman kneeling in a bed of the most beautiful pink flowers. I stopped to ask what they were. "Poppy mallow," she said, and offered me some rootlets for my garden. That was how my friendship with Ginny began. We exchanged plants over the years until she retired and moved to Oregon. I have many plants in my garden to remember her by.

Favorite plants from childhood or from books you've read and enjoyed are also ways to bring the past into your present-day garden. Plants in memory of someone who has died can be a comfort and a way to keep that person's memory alive.

On the day a cousin of mine died after a lengthy illness, I planted a Japanese flowering crab apple tree of the variety Floribunda in my front yard. Each February, close to the anniversary of her death, when the tree comes into its spring bloom and its branches are abundant with pale pink flowers, I feel her presence. She was a person of grace and beauty, and I like to think she would approve of the way I have chosen to memorialize her.

Aside from the utilitarian aspects of restoring, there are aesthetics to be considered. We are imperiled not only by the catastrophes of air and groundwater pollution, acid rain, and the greenhouse effect. Our spirits wither in cities where most architectural design and urban planning are sterile and monotonous.

In conserving and restoring trees and plants, we ensure the preservation of the diverse and exquisite forms in which Nature manifests itself. We keep alive the beauty and wonder of Nature essential to inspiration and our souls' survival.

There is an old Persian saying: "If thou hast two pennies, with one buy bread, with the other, hyacinths for the soul."

Reflecting on Catastrophe and Loss for Emotional and Spiritual Balance

It's time once again to pay a visit to your Mind Garden. Find a quiet place where you can relax, put aside practical concerns, and be with yourself. Take some deep breaths and focus on releasing the tension from your body. As you begin to feel at one with your inner rhythm, take the path that leads to your garden sanctuary.

On your arrival, find a favorite spot where you can rest for a while. Inhale the smell of the sun-warmed soil and the perfume of flowers. Listen to the sound of the wind as it rustles the leaves and sense the teeming life in the earth beneath you.

As you look around, notice the changes that have taken place in the garden since your last visit. Have plants been lost to storm or disease? What trees or shrubs have died?

Take stock of the empty spaces. Think about what you'd like to plant in their place. What would be the best way for you to restore what's been lost? Would you like to revise your garden plan and grow new things, or would you like to replace the lost plants with identical ones? Perhaps you aren't yet ready to fill the empty spaces.

As you think about the losses in your garden, reflect on the losses you are mourning in your life. Are there lingering feelings of grief from the past, perhaps from childhood? Or is the source of your sorrow fresh and recent? Are you still working on accepting the loss?

It's important not to pressure yourself. You need time to work through acceptance of the loss, progressing through the stages of mourning at your own pace.

Perhaps you're done with grieving and are ready to move on. As you go about your daily activities, you will gradually bury your sorrow and find new energy. The cycle of loss and regeneration is an eternal one. Finding our own way to meet these experiences is one of our greatest challenges.

REMEMBERING PAUL

TODAY THE FIRST sweet pea opened. It was a red one that reseeded itself from last year. It made me think of Paul.

Last April, just after the purple-headed iris faded, the sweet peas that draped the picket fence along the east side of the house came into bloom and took their turn as the focal point of the front garden.

They were especially striking as the seed mixture contained a few red ones that had intertwined themselves among the mass of white, pink, and lavender vines.

It was these sweet peas that drew the attention of a slender young man who stopped to look at my garden one morning as I was weeding. "The red ones are my favorites," he said.

He introduced himself to me as a fellow gardener, and in a moment we were talking about a myriad of garden subjects. He told me that he gardened in the backyard of a little house he rented on the other side of town near the beach.

As he spoke of his love of gardening, particularly of his enthusiasm for daffodils, of which he had planted over a hundred that winter, I was struck by the peculiar intensity of his large blue eyes and by the urgency in his tone.

We talked of how wonderfully restorative gardening was—of how much it did for us. He said cryptically, "It's done so much for me—I could tell you terrible things that happened to me in San Francisco before I came here two years ago. My garden is my life. It's how I keep my sanity." He went no further, and I didn't press him.

After a few minutes he looked at his watch and said he'd be late for work if he didn't leave. We said good-bye and I told him that if he liked, when the sweet peas went to seed, I'd harvest some red ones for him.

"I pass this way often on my way to work. I walk from the bus terminal near here," he said, pointing in the direction from which he had come. "I'll be seeing you again."

The next morning I found a potted seedling on my doorstep. A hand-lettered label taped to the side of the plastic container said, "Russell's lupine." It was a plant he'd spoken of the day before, one that I wasn't familiar with.

I didn't have time to put it in the ground, and I set the pot in the garden thinking I'd get to it the next day. But during the night a snail devoured it, and only a truncated stem remained when I looked for it the following morning.

For the next several months, I saw Paul about half a dozen times as he passed on his way to work. Once, in June, he invited himself to lunch and brought his own in a brown paper bag. We sat on my back patio and shared garden news. Again I noted the same intense quality as he spoke of his garden.

In August when the sweet peas had gone to seed and the pods had dried, I picked some and put them in an envelope and wrote Paul's name on it. But I didn't see him during the fall and winter. I tried calling him a few times, but no one answered. At Christmas I sent him a card, and then, in January, he knocked on my door. He was thinner than before and looked drawn and tired.

"I've come to let you know that this was my last day of work. My illness has made me too weak to continue. I have AIDS." He said the word quickly as though that would lessen its impact and then went on, "I wanted to thank you for your card and your friendship. I probably won't be coming this way for a while."

I asked him if he'd like to come in. He thanked me but said he was on his way to a doctor's appointment. We said we'd get together soon.

The following week I visited Paul at his home, an old beach cottage two blocks from the ocean. The interior was airy and light. Sun streamed through uncurtained windows on the west side of the house and through an open door to the rear of the house that led to the garden.

Except for a mattress on the bedroom floor and a table and chairs in the kitchen, there was no furniture. Clothes, books, magazines, and papers were neatly stacked in piles on the floor in the living room and bedroom, as though since his arrival he'd been prepared to leave on short notice.

On the floor next to the refrigerator stood a large, rectangular animal cage in which lay a listless, gray tabby cat. On a table next to it sat a smaller cage that housed a pair of finches, which leapt and fluttered excitedly from perch to perch as we came into the room. Paul explained that the birds had been a gift from a friend.

"He has leukemia," he said, pointing to the cat. "I got him from the pound. I went there looking for a pet, and he was there. I just couldn't let them put him to death." He gestured and cooed affectionately at the languishing animal, but it stared straight ahead and didn't move.

Paul was even thinner than before. (The word "emaciated" came to mind. I pushed it away.) His trousers hung loosely from his waist, and his leather belt had been tightened to gather in a waistband that had been too large for quite some time. Now the belt was buckled on its last hole, and the end of it, showing several worn holes, dangled to one side.

His eyes, sunk deeply into their sockets, were still lively, and during a tour of the backyard, he gestured animatedly as he described his plantings.

A few bulbs had begun to push up from the ground, but there wasn't much in flower. Although it was a California garden and could have been resplendent with winter bloom, Paul had put all of his energies into planting for spring.

On the way into the house, Paul turned to a half-empty sack of bulbs sitting open on a bench on the back porch. "I have more of these King Alfred daffodils than I can use. I want to plant some in your garden," he said.

After our visit, I took him to lunch at a restaurant that served Indonesian food, which he'd never eaten before. He scanned the foreign-sounding menu with curiosity, made a few tentative choices, and then after asking the waiter to explain the contents of these dishes, decided on a chicken dish with peanut sauce. He ate it with his usual gusto.

I never saw him again. During the next couple of weeks, I tried several times to reach him by phone but no one answered. Then one day in February I tried again. A man answered and told me Paul was in the hospital. I called the number he gave me. The phone rang and rang but no one answered.

The next morning I called the hospital and asked for Paul Hunter. The operator said no patient was listed by that name.

I felt a foreboding and phoned his home again. This time a woman answered. She asked who I was. I told her that Paul and I were gardening friends. She paused, as though scanning a mental directory of those that could be privy to the secret she held. Deciding in my favor, she went on, "This is his sister. Paul died last night."

She said his family was distributing his plants and asked if I wanted anything. I told her about the King Alfred daffodil bulbs. She took my name and number, but I never heard from her.

Funny how memories of people become attached to things. I'll never see a red sweet pea without thinking of Paul. Each spring, I'll watch for them to sprout along the side-yard fence. When they do, I'll think of a garden on the other side of town awash with yellow King Alfred daffodils.

9

HARVESTING

So instead of getting to Heaven, at last—

I'm going, all along.

EMILY DICKINSON

H

ARVEST—THE WORD IT-
self, spoken like a sigh, tells us we've come to a point of
completion. Through our constancy and care, the seeds
we've guided through a season of growth have ripened and
borne flowers and fruit.

In the shimmer of an August afternoon, I sit in the
shade on my front porch savoring the lush ripeness of my
sun-washed garden. Today, it seems that Nature has put the
last stroke to its summer canvas. Color, shape, and scent
conspire to bring my garden to the peak of summer bloom.

The Peruvian lilies have flowered, and the last of the
salmon-pink gladiolus opened this morning. Four yellow
Peace roses are in full bloom. Clusters of zinnias, asters, carnations, and marigolds have woven themselves into a vivid
garden brocade of pink, blue, red, and yellow.

A breeze stirs the flowers and sends a heady mixture of
the scent of roses and carnations wafting upward to where I
sit. I inhale the sweet, rich aroma while relaxing to the mes-
merizing hum of flies and bees.

Garden and gardener have come full cycle. I am flooded
with feelings of joy and fulfillment as the garden I dreamed
of, planned, and worked for through the past several
months has come into full flowering. It's a splendid moment, deeply gratifying in many ways. I luxuriate in the satisfaction of having acted in concert with Nature, of having
understood my own needs and those of my garden plants—
of having held onto the vision of how my garden could be
and persevered as I cleared, dug, planted, and tended.

If my garden were a farm and my flowers a food crop, I would be hard at work harvesting everything. But here, on this warm summer day, I harvest with my senses and my thoughts rather than my hands. When I do harvest my flowers, I pick carefully and selectively—an armful of roses to fill a vase or a mixed bouquet to give to a friend. I want to enjoy and preserve the beauty of this lush fruiting and flowering for as long as possible.

Sometimes we don't remember to pause and enjoy the harvests in our lives. We become accustomed to the steady momentum of routines directed toward our goals and lose sight of the fact that we've come to a point of completion. It's important to stop for a moment, to rest and celebrate. We undergo an adjustment as the end of a cycle of work nears. We stop putting out energy, pause, and take in our accomplishments, reaping the fruits of our labor.

Harvest of the Small

While each of the garden's seasonal harvests brings a deep sense of satisfaction, the garden is always giving returns. The attentive gardener knows that she or he harvests daily, not just when flowers are in full bloom. In each moment there is a harvest.

We need to recognize and appreciate the harvest of the small. These are the simple things that delight the senses and soothe the spirit: satisfaction in digging and turning the earth for some new plants; joy in noticing that a dry little seed you buried just days before has broken through the soil; pride and a sense of accomplishment as planting beds, shrubs, and trees offer a profusion of color, pleasing scents and shapes.

We can take pleasure in the small tasks and routines that help our gardens along. Muscles and joints you haven't used for a long time may at first feel stiff and sore as you stoop and bend to weed and dig. But in a short while, as your body opens to new movement and activity, you'll feel invigorated, stronger, and more limber.

Each day the garden offers something new: the taste of the first ripe strawberry of the season, the smell of orange blossoms on a sunny afternoon, the iridescence of a dragonfly's wings. The naturalist John Burroughs said, "To find new things, take the path you took yesterday."

In the cycles of life, like the cycles of the garden, we plant, grow, and harvest many times. In the course of living a full life, we have many gardens in progress. We ourselves go through transformations similar to the ones we encourage in the garden.

Awareness of the ongoing processes of our various life gardens will enable us to reap the harvest of the small.

The most successful and lasting harvest is a blending of the two harvests—the dramatic one that culminates in baskets of plump, golden apricots or a handful of daffodils and the daily one in which we reap ongoing rewards.

Surprise Harvest

Each harvest is different. So many factors determine the outcome of our plantings: the care we give, the quality of the seed, the soil, the amount of rainfall, the temperature range of a particular growing season. Sometimes I get more than expected, and sometimes I get less.

A new rhododendron puts forth an astonishing number of pink blooms during its first season. A burgundy-colored iris with a fuzzy, yellow throat appears unexpectedly in a bed of pale lavender ones.

Along the length of fence that separates my neighbor's garden from mine, I've noticed some flowers I didn't plant: wild geraniums with scalloped leaves and little purple blooms, tiny chrysanthemums called feverfew, with clusters of yellow-centered white flowers and a spicy aroma. While it's reassuring to know that I can plan my garden and grow and harvest the flowers I want, it's reaffirming, too, that despite all of my attempts at control, Nature adds its own ideas to my garden scheme. I'm reminded that I'm part of a larger process.

Invisible Harvest

Occasionally as I plant and tend my garden, I feel twinges of guilt. An old voice within tells me I should be doing something more useful with my time, that spending my energies in the garden is self-centered and self-indulgent. But I know as I survey the beauty and fruitfulness before me that it was first necessary for me to focus on this one particular space in order to grasp the significance that making and keeping a garden can have for everyone.

Gardening can provide us with a model of how we want to live. The sense of balance and wholeness it gives, the ethos of nurturance and caring for all living things it fosters ripple outward in ever-widening circles to touch the lives of friends, family, and community. Gardening gives meaning and force to the phrase *healing the planet*.

The generosity of gardeners is legendary. The excitement of sharing and exchanging with friends the plants we've grown and harvested is a personal and creative pleasure that can't be matched by purchased gifts. Not only do I have the memory of the fresh taste of the ripe plums and the smell of the little bouquet of roses that a neighbor brought when I was ill but she also shared with me the love and caring that she had put into these growing things.

Long after the harvest we hold in our hands is gone, we are left with the one in our hearts and minds—a deeper, more lasting harvest. Our personal harvest is the knowledge we've acquired, the challenges we've met, the satisfaction we've found along the way. The person who understands the many harvests of experience that gardening offers finds abundance in each day.

Through bringing plants to maturity, we learn step by step what it takes to grow something and nurture it to fruition. We can think of our dreams as the seeds of possibilities that the ways of the garden can help us realize. We can apply the cumulative wisdom we've learned from gardening in every aspect of our lives. Once we've harvested, our knowledge of ourselves deepens, and we gain a sense of the proper balance that must be maintained with Nature for personal and global health.

Harvesting for Emotional and Spiritual Balance

Find a quiet place where you can relax and take time for yourself. Close your eyes and take a few deep breaths. For the next few moments, continue to breathe deeply, calming yourself as you release the tensions that have been building within. When you feel ready, find your way to your Mind Garden.

When you arrive, look around you and see what is ready to be harvested. As you see the Canterbury bells, marguerites, and larkspur in full bloom and the apple and pear trees you planted ripe with fruit, feel your pride and sense of accomplishment in bringing them from seed and seedling to maturity. With loving care, diligence, and patience you've nurtured and guided your garden from planting to fruiting and flowering. Your mindful tending has brought you a harvest of health and beauty.

Think of the pure oxygen that the delicate, feathered leaves on the jacaranda tree and the green fronds of the bird's-nest fern are putting out into the atmosphere. Take a deep breath and inhale this harvest of freshness. In making your garden, you've not only enriched the soil but you've helped to cleanse the air around you.

Think of how much more in touch you are with your true needs as a result of cutting back and weeding out the extraneous in your life. As you've pruned away the excess and rooted out the unnecessary in your garden, your own personal priorities have become clearer.

Think of how you've increased your ability to finish what you start. As you've guided and followed your garden from planting to harvesting, you've developed the patience and perseverance essential to bringing your own plans to fruition.

Give yourself ample time to reflect on all you've accomplished through spending time in your garden. This is a moment when you can truly "rest on your laurels." It really doesn't matter whether your garden is small and simple or large and elaborate—each thing you've grown is a little harvest unto itself that has taught you something.

Feel the deep sense of affirmation of your own life and of life on the planet that your garden provides.

What you have harvested during this growing season will be of lasting value. If, under the pressures and demands of daily life, your Mind Garden begins to slip away and the colors, scents, and sounds begin to fade, remember that within easy reach, only a breath or two away, is an oasis of rest and peace that can lead you back to Nature. Here is a place where you can clear, dig, plant, grow, and harvest—the life garden of your mind.

10

GLEANINGS

To hope for Paradise is to live in Paradise.

VITA SACKVILLE–WEST

FROM THE BEGINNING OF recorded time, societies have shared the universal myth of paradise as a garden. The very word *paradise* comes from an old Persian word *pairidaeza,* which means walled garden.

Throughout the centuries, each culture has invented its own version of Eden. Egyptian tomb paintings depict garden retreats graced with leafy trees, flowers, and pools of water. The early Romans worshiped Nature deities such as the goddess Flora and made square or oblong outdoor garden rooms planted with grape vines, fruit trees, and roses. The Japanese used water, stone, trees, and rocks to create landscapes that symbolized Nature and the mysterious forces of the universe. No matter what images each culture chose, they included trees and flowers, and they stressed harmony with Nature.

Nostalgia and yearning for a return to a place of perfect peace and plenty persist today. But as natural resources are drained, pollution spreads, and vast areas of the earth's forests are destroyed, it is increasingly difficult to sustain a vision of paradise.

The world has changed and become more and more complex. We can't go back to our old image of Eden. We need a new vision—one that embodies the ideals of the past, the realities of the present, and our hopes for the future.

As we've walked through the garden in this book, we can see that the wisdom we need in order to create this vision is right here before us. In my own garden, I've seen how each tender shoot, each full blossom, and each with-ered leaf play a role in the harmony and survival of the garden as a whole.

In my own life, I've seen how the garden's wisdom teaches me how to survive. The problems and obstacles I face and the disappointments and losses I experience are as important to my balance and well-being as my joys and successes.

We need to break ground for a new world garden. We need to view the earth's resources in terms of long-term care, thinking the way a gardener thinks, with the future in mind, preparing for the cycles of growth yet to come.

With Nature the centerpiece of our lives and with technology to serve and support it, we can create harmony and peace here, not in the hereafter. We don't have to fantasize about it—we can do it. It's within our power. In the world's survival lies our own immortality.

The garden is a living testament for our children.

It will tell them whether we really cared. A Kenyan proverb says, "Treat the earth well. It was not given to you by your parents. It was lent to you by your children."

APPENDIX

America the Beautiful Fund
  Department CE
219 Shoreham Building NW
Washington, DC 20005
(202) 638–1649
A national nonprofit organization helping volunteers save the
natural and human-made beauty
of America. To receive information on applying for a grant of
free seeds to start a community
garden, send a stamped self-
addressed envelope.

American Community
  Gardening Association
325 Walnut Street
Philadelphia, PA 19106
(215) 625–8280
A nonprofit membership organization of gardening and open-
space volunteers and professionals
that promotes the growth of
community gardening and
greening in urban, suburban, and
rural America. Members work
with community groups and
public agencies to establish community gardens, parks, and other
green spaces.

American Horticultural
  Therapy Association
9220 Wightman Road,
  Suite 300
Gaithersburg, MD 20879
(301) 948–3010
A nonprofit membership organization that promotes the use
of gardening as a therapeutic
aid. Professionals and volunteers
provide access to gardening for
the rehabilitation of disabled
and disadvantaged persons.

Center for Psychology
  and Social Change
1493 Cambridge Street
Cambridge, MA 02139
An affiliate of the Harvard
Medical School that explores
ways to promote shifts in con-
sciousness and behavior that invite sustainable, equitable, and
peaceful ways of living.

Life Lab Science Program
1156 High Street
Santa Cruz, CA 95064
(408) 459–2001
Students learn by doing in this

hands-on approach to elementary school science. The curriculum integrates life, earth, and physical sciences and uses a school-based garden as a living laboratory to demonstrate how an ecosystem works. Life Lab offers various materials and in-service training to teachers and schools interested in implementing its program.

Master Gardeners'
  International Corporation
  (MaGIC)
2904 Cameron Mills Road
Alexandria, VA 22302
(703) 683–6485
MaGIC is a membership organization made up of Master Gardeners, volunteers trained by the Cooperative Extension Service of the U.S. Department of Agriculture, who work within their communities to promote the benefits of gardening and home horticulture. MaGIC distributes information and publishes a directory that lists the more than 600 Master Gardener training programs throughout the United States and Canada.

National Gardening
  Association
180 Flynn Avenue
Burlington, VT 05401
(802) 863–1308
A nonprofit membership organization that encourages and supports gardening and develops elementary science and environmental programs for young people. The association also publishes a bimonthly magazine and produces books and videos about gardening.

People-Plant Council
c/o Virginia Polytechnic
  Institute & State University
Blacksburg, VA 24061–0327
(703) 231–6254
An interdisciplinary group of educators, researchers, businesses, professionals, volunteers, and amateurs that uses education, networking, and research to establish and promote the relationship between plants and human well-being.

SELECTED BIBLIOGRAPHY

Butterfly Gardening: Creating Summer Magic in Your Garden. Created by the Xerces Society in association with the Smithsonian Institution. Sierra Club Books, San Francisco, in association with the National Wildlife Federation, Washington, D.C., 1990.

Cowell, F. R. *The Garden as a Fine Art: From Antiquity to Modern Times.* Houghton Mifflin Company: Boston, 1991.

Cox, Jeff. *Landscaping with Nature—Using Nature's Designs to Plan Your Yard.* Rodale Press: Emmaus, PA, 1991.

Cox, Jeff, and Jerry Pavia. *Creating a Garden for the Senses.* Abbeville Press Publishers: New York, 1993.

Dennis, John V. *The Wildlife Gardener: How to create a pleasing garden that will be a mecca for all manner of wildlife from birds, bees, and butterflies to small mammals, reptiles, and amphibians.* Alfred Knopf: New York, 1985.

Ernst, Ruth Shaw. *The Naturalist's Garden.* Rodale Press: Emmaus, PA, 1987.

The Gardener's Palette: The Ultimate Garden Plant Planner. Designed and produced by the Rainbird Publishing Group Doubleday: New York, 1986.

Harper, Peter, with Chris Madsen and Jeremy Light. *The Natural Garden Book: A Holistic Approach to Gardening.* Gaia Books/Simon & Schuster Inc.: New York, 1994.

Messervy, Julie Moir. *The Inward Garden: Creating a Place of Beauty and Meaning.* Little, Brown and Company: Boston, MA, 1995.

Ocone, Lynne, and Eve Pranis. *National Gardening Association's Guide to Kids' Gardening.* National Gardening Association: Burlington, VT, 1990.

Oechsli, Helen, and Kelly Oechsli. *In My Garden: A Child's Gardening Book.* MacMillan Publishing Company: New York, 1985.

Rodale's Chemical-Free Yard & Garden: The Ultimate Authority on Successful Organic Gardening. Edited by Fern M. Bradley. Rodale Press: Emmaus, PA, 1991.

Roth, Susan A. *The Weekend Garden Guide: Work-Saving Ways to a Beautiful Backyard.* Rodale Press: Emmaus, PA, 1991.

Rothert, Gene. *The Enabling Garden: A Guide to Lifelong Gardening.* Taylor Publishing Company: Dallas, TX, 1994 (for people with disabilities and older adults).

Seed Savers Exchange: The First Ten Years 1975–1985. Edited by Kent Whealy and Arllys Adelmann. Seed Saver Publications: Decorah, IA, 1986.

Sommers, Larry. *The Community Garden Book.* National Gardening Association: Burlington, VT, 1978–1980.

Stein, Sarah. *Noah's Garden: Restoring the Ecology of Our Own Back Yards.* Houghton Mifflin Company: New York, 1993.

Stevenson, Violet. *The Wild Garden: Making Natural Gardens Using Wild and Native Plants.* Penguin Handbook. Viking Penguin Inc.: New York, 1985.

Taylor, Norman. *Taylor's Guide to Water-Saving Gardening.* Houghton Mifflin Company: Boston, 1990.

Verey, Rosemary. *The Scented Garden.* Random House: New York, 1981.

Wilson, Jim. *Landscaping with Container Plants.* Houghton Mifflin Company: Boston, MA, 1990.

Yang, Linda. *The City Gardener's Handbook: From Balcony to Backyard.* Random House: New York, 1990.